# William Shakespeare's Strange Case of Doctor Jekyll and Mister Hyde

## IAN DOESCHER

Based on the novella by
Robert Louis Stevenson

To Rob and Sarah—full of energy,
compassion, wisdom, hope, and joy.

# DRAMATIS PERSONAE

Gabriel John Utterson, *lawyer and Chorus*

Doctor Henry Jekyll, *or Mister Edward Hyde*
Richard Enfield, *a gentleman*
Doctor Hastie Lanyon, *longtime friend of Jekyll*
Inspector Newcomen, *of Scotland Yard*
Poole, *Jekyll's valet*
Ruth, *Hyde's maid*
Edith, *a woman of London*
Danvers Carew, *Member of Parliament*
Guest, *Utterson's clerk*

A young girl, a doctor, a locksmith, a driver, a flower seller, a messenger, and various citizens.

**Scene:** London

# Prologue.

*Enter GABRIEL JOHN UTTERSON as Chorus.*

Utterson        Twin adversaries held within one soul,
The better and the worser parts of nature,
Which we term good and evil—such are they
O'er which philosophers spill endless ink,
About which all religions spawn beliefs,       5
Twixt which we teach our children to discern.
Yet ne'er was person built who could withstand
The pull of each, which tears the heart in twain,
For all have samplèd virtue's sweet delights,
The honey-kiss'd confection of good deeds,     10
Which, in the doing, falleth on the tongue
Like heav'nly sugar sent from realms above.
And, just as surely, all do know the salt
Of evil deeds, which flavor human life,
Those hidden moments of mouthwat'ring wrong   15
Done in despite of what the world calls right—
The taste of pure, forbidden decadence.
'Tis as Saint Paul hath writ these ages hence:
The good that I would do, I yet do not;
The evil which I would not do, I do.        20
Ne'er hath a person total good achiev'd,
For what the moralists will ne'er admit—
With all their homilies condemning vice,
And claiming for themselves pure righteousness,
Whilst, in the darkness, they make love to sin—   25
Is that the one cannot live sans the other,
No good without its evil, and no vice
Without its virtue, halves of selfsame whole.
Be, then, amaz'd by what shall here unfold,
A tale of one who would his evil purge     30
And separate it bodily from him—

A rift both literal and absolute,
That had th'effect of setting evil free
Upon a city wholly unprepar'd.
Watch how these double faces, Janus-like,   35
Turn back upon each other to their ruin.
Forsooth, events most errant shall betide,
A strange case: Doctor Jekyll, Mister Hyde!

*[Exit.*

# ACT I

## SCENE 1.
### *A laboratory.*

*Enter HENRY JEKYLL, at his instruments.*

| | |
|---|---|
| Jekyll | Tush! Never tell me what may not be done, |
| | For I, this night, compound the very drug |
| | By which my nat'ral body and its pow'rs |
| | Shall be dethron'd from their supremacy, |
| | Another form and countenance assum'd,       5 |
| | Which is no less expression of myself. |

*Enter POOLE.*

| | |
|---|---|
| Poole | Good even, Doctor Jekyll. |
| Jekyll |     —Hoyday, Poole, |
| | I bid thee leave me to my crucial work, |
| | Which risks collapse when interruption comes. |
| Poole | Beg pardon, sir, I only wish'd to ask      10 |
| | If Ruth and I your supper should prepare. |
| Jekyll | No supper, thank you. Prithee, now, be gone, |
| | And close the chamber door as thou depart'st. |
| Poole | Indeed. Best wishes for a fruitful night. |

*[Exit Poole.*

| | |
|---|---|
| Jekyll | Sans further intermission or delay,      15 |
| | I must put theory to the test of practice. |
| | My mind doth hesitate, though, at the thought, |
| | For soon I'll meet my lower elements, |
| | Long captive to the better part of me |

And longing for release which, by this draught,　　20
May give the silent demon in me voice.
Yet in the trial shall I risk my death:
A drug that doth so potently control
And shake the fortress of identity
May by some overdose or misadventure　　25
Blot out the very tabernacle of
My body that I merely hope to alter.
Such mortal drugs I have, but physic's law
Is death to any he that would misuse them.
Take courage, Jekyll—many are the days　　30
O'er which thou hast prepar'd thy tincture rare.

*[He prepares the potion.*

Compound the elements, bring them to boil,
Watch how they smoke together in the glass,
Now prove that thou believest in thy toil.

*[He drinks.*

O, awful pangs come o'er me in a trice!　　35
A grinding in the bones as known by those
Who face their torture on the dreaded rack,
A deadly nausea in my belly worse
Than when one first doth journey on the sea.
Most foul of all, a horror in my spirit　　40
Unknown e'en at the hour of birth or death.
My body changeth, I can feel 'tis so—
A looking-glass! A looking-glass at once!

*[He finds a mirror behind his equipment. He cannot be seen by the audience as*
*he looks at his reflection.*

What have I done? What shall I come to do?

*[Exit.*


*Enter POOLE and RUTH.*


Ruth　　　　　Will our good master come for supper, Poole?　　45

| | |
|---|---|
| Poole | Nay, for he burns the midnight oil within<br>His lab'ratory. |
| Ruth | —Such hath been his wont<br>Too many nights of late. I fear me for<br>His health, which needs must suffer for his work. |
| Poole | I'll warrant thou hast reason for thy fear. 50 |
| Ruth | I'll warrant thou dost fear he sees not reason. |
| Poole | Troth, Ruth, for in my years of serving him<br>I never have beheld him so engag'd,<br>So focus'd on his labors that he doth<br>Ignore the comforts of his daily life. 55<br>The man is like an arrow in its flight,<br>Releasèd from an expert archer's bow<br>And sailing swiftly to its destin'd target. |
| Ruth | We must hope that the one who aims, aims well,<br>Toward some worthy end and not to ill. 60 |
| Poole | Such is our hope. Let us abide in it. |

*Enter HENRY JEKYLL.*

| | |
|---|---|
| Jekyll | Good even, loyal Poole and precious Ruth. |
| Poole | Well met, sir, though the nightingale sings. |
| Jekyll | Is there yet aught of supper I may taste?<br>Although I did refuse the proffer'd meal, 65<br>Mine appetite is changèd suddenly. |

Ruth        It shall be done, and does my spirit well
            To see you are inclin'd to break your fast.

                                      [*She begins to leave, to get his supper.*

Jekyll      Ere thou dost go, Ruth, I must have a word.

Ruth        Your will, sir?

Jekyll              —Soon, a man of mine acquaintance        70
            Shall come to live nearby. He is a friend—
            [*Aside:*] Nay, more than that, more like a brother he,
            Or like the other half of mine own self—
            [*Aloud:*] And he requires a housemaid of discretion,
            One who hath skill and circumspection both,        75
            One who hath prov'd herself a loyal help,
            One who could never be replac'd.

Ruth                —Methinks
            You mean to flatter, sir, when you may order.

Jekyll      I shall not order thee to take the post,
            Should it be past the bounds of thine own will.     80

Ruth        For years, your steadfast will hath been mine own.
            If you would have me serve this friend of yours,
            I'll gladly undertake to serve him well.

Jekyll      And for the deed thou hast my many thanks.

Ruth        May I, sir, ask how long the man shall need         85
            My services? For though I shall endeavor
            To treat him, Doctor Jekyll, as yourself,
            I know my heart will long to be back home
            And shall be restless until I return.

Jekyll      Dear Ruth, thou art as constant as the sun.      90
                My friend shall come to stay a little while
                And shall assist me in my private work.
                Let us say six months at the uttermost.
                *[Aside:]* Though I fear this may be a time too brief
                To have all matters answer'd to my mind.      95

Ruth        It shall be done, sir, even as you say.

Jekyll      Come, let us toast the dawning of the day.

                                           *[Exeunt Jekyll and Poole.*

Ruth        Another man my master bids me serve,
                And though my wishes like the duty not,
                In all things shall I be obedient,      100
                For truly Doctor Jekyll is a man
                Of most uncommon virtue, known throughout
                All London as a noble, upright sort,
                Whose charity to those less fortunate
                Is recogniz'd by all and much esteem'd,      105
                Whose temperament is generous and kind
                To any whom he meeteth, high or low,
                Whose contributions to the common good
                Through his employment bring him great renown.
                Such is my master. Thus, since he doth bid,      110
                To serve my master's friend shall be my joy,
                For any friend of Doctor Jekyll's must
                Be one in whom I may vouchsafe my trust.

                                               *[Exit.*

## SCENE 2.
### *A street. Night.*

*Enter a YOUNG GIRL.*

Girl                  La! Three o'clock or later falls the hour,
Yet home doth beckon, still some miles away.
So dark a street on such a frosty night
I ne'er did travel 'pon. These yellow lamps,
Which light the way with flames like burnish'd gold,    5
Are all the signs I see of human life—
The produce of the one who taketh care
To light the lamps for trav'lers such as I.
Lamplighters all, my thanks: you lead me home.

*Enter EDWARD HYDE, a man short of stature, crossing near the GIRL.*

Hyde               *[aside:]* A night most dark for even darker deeds.    10
Upon whom shall I ply my vice tonight?

*[In their haste, the girl and Hyde run into each other. She falls.*

Girl                  Apologies, good sir.

Hyde                       —Insensate wretch!
Thou shalt an answer make for crossing me!

*[He begins to stomp on her.*

Girl                  Help, ho! I am attack'd! Help, or I die!

*Enter RICHARD ENFIELD, a DOCTOR, and another CITIZEN.*

Doctor            What evil's this? Release her, scoundrel vile!    15

*[Hyde stands aside. The doctor kneels over the girl.*

Hyde            These tramps deserve their trampling, by my troth.
                Yea, such foul dirt belongeth underfoot.

Enfield         Thy name shall dirt become for this misdeed,
                The dirt on thee shall spread throughout all London.
                *[Aside:]* What horror, even to behold this man—        20
                There's aught within his countenance to make
                E'en Hercules forsake his labors twelve.

Citizen 1       What is thy name?

Hyde                        —Such knowledge thou earn'st not,
                Yet I shall tell thee, for in time thou mayst—
                Indeed, ye all may—come to fear its sound:              25
                My name is Edward Hyde.

Enfield         *[aside:]* —My soul could not
                Be more afeard had he said Lucifer.

Citizen 1       I see, sir, that you bear a doctor's touch,
                The gentleness and skill with which thou treat'st
                Thy young and batter'd patient's evident.              30
                How doth she fare?

Doctor                      —She shall recover soon;
                She suffers less from injury than fear,
                Though had we not been near enow, I trow
                We should have found the lady a grave lass.
                *[Aside:]* I do confess that, were I doctor none—       35
                Were I not sworn by oath life to protect,
                And do no harm in practicing my trade—
                I'd gladly slay this beastly little man.

| | |
|---|---|
| Enfield | *[to Hyde:]* I, sirrah, am so bold as to declare |
| | That thou must make some restitution swift.     40 |
| | We three bore witness to barbarity |
| | Of such degree as would thy name destroy, |
| | Should it be broadly known what thou hast done |
| | Unto an innocent and harmless lady. |
| | |
| Hyde | What restitution shall this urchin make     45 |
| | For flitting to and fro throughout the street— |
| | Like one entirely lacking common sense— |
| | And running headlong into gentlemen? |
| | |
| Citizen 1 | Thou hast not proven thyself gentle, sirrah, |
| | Yet thou mayst still be called a man an thou     50 |
| | Wilt take responsibility herein |
| | And make a worthy recompense to her. |
| | |
| Doctor | By God, we'll see thee ruin'd otherwise. |
| | |
| Hyde | I see you three have turn'd triumvirate |
| | Like Antony, Octavius, and Lepidus,     55 |
| | And cast me in the role of lawless brute. |
| | Since ye present a greater force than I— |
| | *[Aside:]* Though I am tempted to engage ye still— |
| | *[Aloud:]* And threaten action o'er this accident |
| | I am, thus, render'd helpless natur'lly.     60 |
| | No gentleman but wishes to avoid |
| | A scene. I shall bequeath this trifling soul |
| | Some meager portion of the fortune vast |
| | Which I do hold in trust for mine own use. |
| | This door is mine, bills of exchange within—     65 |
| | Give me some moments few and ye shall have |
| | The ransom you unjustly do demand. |

*[Exit Hyde to one of the doors.*

Girl            My thanks, sirs, for your aid in this event,
                         Which shaketh me no less than quake of earth.

Doctor         Rest, lass, and we shall see thee safely home         70
                         Once this unworthy man hath paid his due.

Girl            To bid him make a reparation was
                         Not in my thoughts. You do me too kind service—
                         Escaping with my life is payment full.

Citizen 1     He shall make restitution and be glad;               75
                         He doth deserve a harsher punishment,
                         And any funds he gives thee is a price
                         Too little when compar'd to liberty,
                         For, truly, he should end this night in jail.

*Enter EDWARD HYDE.*

Hyde           Take thou the hearty sum of fifty pounds,        80
                         And be thou grateful that assistance came
                         And I had not the opportunity
                         To finish well what I began, rash wench.

Enfield        Wilt thou continue in thy wickedness?
                         Give me the bill and I shall give it her,          85
                         For thou shalt not approach her one step more
                         Unless thou wouldst our harsher tempers face.

*[Hyde hands Enfield the bill of exchange, which Enfield scans before handing*
*to the girl.*

Doctor         Now get thee gone and darken not these streets.

Hyde           *[aside:]* Would we could meet again, I'd make thee eat
                         The valiant, hasty words thou darest speak.        90

*[Exit Hyde.*

Citizen 1      *[to Girl:]* Now, let us get thee safely to thy home;
               We shall accompany thee on thy way.

Girl           The journey is yet long, the hour grows later.
               I could not ask ye for such courtesy.

Doctor         Thou need'st not ask, the favor is our own.        95
               *[To Enfield:]* Wilt thou go with us three, sir?

Enfield                —Presently.
               Pray, lead the way, and I shall follow on.
                              *[Exeunt girl, doctor, and citizen.*
               Most unexpected, strange, and curious—
               The bill the scoundrel render'd to the girl
               Appear'd legitimate on fleeting glance,            100
               Yet it was drawn upon th'account of one
               Of our most upright, blameless citizens,
               His signature upon the bill emblazon'd!
               Will this horrific man I met tonight—
               Who seems to me more hellish imp than man—         105
               Add forgery unto his battery?
               Come morn, I'll call upon the commerce house
               Inquiring whether 'twas a counterfeit,
               And soon reveal this mystery peculiar.
               I'll warrant my suspicion falls not wide—          110
               There's yet more menace in this Mister Hyde.

                                                        *[Exit.*

## SCENE 3.
### *A street.*

*Enter GABRIEL JOHN UTTERSON.*

| | |
|---|---|
| Utterson | What better prospect for an autumn morn— |
| | When nighttime's rain transforms to sunshine's rays, |
| | When phantoms of the dark give way to light— |
| | Than this: the promise of a Sunday walk, |
| | My habit with my priz'd friend, Mister Enfield,     5 |
| | Who hath provided constant company |
| | For many years on Sundays such as these. |

*Enter RICHARD ENFIELD.*

| | |
|---|---|
| Enfield | Holla, dear Utterson! |

| | |
|---|---|
| Utterson |     —What ho, my friend. |
| | Art ready for another Sunday stroll? |

| | |
|---|---|
| Enfield | If these two legs will carry my poor frame     10 |
| | Despite th'events that happ'd these six days past, |
| | I am prepar'd to wander where thou wilt. |

*[They begin walking.*

| | |
|---|---|
| Utterson | Such strange allusions frame your confirmation, |
| | That thou—like fishmonger who spears a worm, |
| | Producing bait, and shall, when all is done,     15 |
| | Eat of the fish that hath fed of that worm— |
| | Hast caught me quite. What tidings wouldst thou tell? |

| | |
|---|---|
| Enfield | 'Twas late on Monday—early Tuesday, rather, |
| | For well past midnight's chime the clock was run. |
| | My evening had mix'd vice and virtue both,     20 |

> In perfect combination built for pleasure—

Utterson     Thou ever wert a brazen epicure.

Enfield      I do confess. Yet, by this story's end,
             I'll wager I shall sport an angel's wings,
             For thou shalt know one far more devilish.          25

Utterson     To view thee as angelic would amaze,
             For that I know thy truer, baser nature.
             Proceed, then, with thy tale.

Enfield                       —Round three o'clock,
             Two other men and I, the three of us
             All travelers, by chance, of one same road,         30
             Came on a short and trollish-looking man
             As he did stomp upon a poor, young woman.

Utterson     Stomp on her, didst thou say? O, surely not.

Enfield      No other word could match his actions rude,
             She there upon the ground and he above,             35
             His feet a-trouncing o'er her little frame
             As if she were aflame and he could quell it.

Utterson     Yet wherefore did he so?

Enfield                       —As well might thou
             Bid of a dog why it doth bark and bite:
             Methinks it is the man's malicious nature           40
             And that alone.

Utterson                      —What did you do, thou and
             The other two who journey'd on their way?

| Enfield | We shouted at him, bidding him to stop, |
|---|---|
| | Which, with resistance and much discontent, |
| | He was persuaded, finally, to do. 45 |
| | Yet, for the evil deed, we bid him give |
| | Some sum of pounds unto the frighten'd girl— |
| | Who, thankfully, was not too gravely hurt— |
| | And though 'twas clear he would much rather flee, |
| | We three were bound to make him pay amends. 50 |

| Utterson | Well reason'd—price too low for public menace. |
|---|---|

| Enfield | Quite so. We were, by hap, quite near his home. |
|---|---|
| | Thus he produc'd a key and went within, |
| | So to produce the necessary bill. |
| | When he did give it her, I saw the name 55 |
| | Upon which his full fifty pounds were drawn— |
| | A name I shall not mention, yet which is |
| | Well-known and often on the public tongue. |

| Utterson | E'en so? And thinkest thou 'twas genuine? |
|---|---|

| Enfield | The next day, I inquir'd unto the bank, 60 |
|---|---|
| | Whereon the man's bill of exchange was drawn. |
| | I'd reason to believe 'twas forgery, |
| | Yet not a bit of it. 'Twas genuine. |

| Utterson | Tut-tut! |
|---|---|

| Enfield | —Thou feelest even as I do. |
|---|---|
| | The fellow was a beast, with whom none should 65 |
| | Associate, a man most damnable, |
| | Whilst he who drew the funds is one of our |
| | Most celebrated, honor'd citizens, |
| | Of whom all good is thought, and evil none. |

| | | |
|---|---|---|
| Utterson | Belike a case of slander, I suspect. | 70 |
| | An honest man who payeth frequently | |
| | For some odd misadventure of his youth. | |
| | | |
| Enfield | Yea, such was my assessment of the case. | |
| | | |
| Utterson | Art thou most certain he, whose funds they are, | |
| | Lives not within this house the rogue did enter? | 75 |
| | | |
| Enfield | Nay, I know of the worthy man's address— | |
| | 'Tis in the neighborhood, but not this house. | |
| | Pray, listen on: since then, I have made study | |
| | Of that same dwelling where the brigand vile | |
| | Doth make his home. It scarcely seems a house— | 80 |
| | None use the door except the gentleman | |
| | (A word I loosely use) of my adventure. | |
| | Although the smoke that from the chimney rises | |
| | Bears witness to the resident within, | |
| | There are no other signs of human life— | 85 |
| | The hurly-burly of the common household— | |
| | In evidence. | |
| | | |
| Utterson | —One question more, I pray: | |
| | How did this man appear? Thou didst refer | |
| | To him as trollish-looking. Such a phrase, | |
| | Which sparks contempt in the imagination, | 90 |
| | Must be an overstatement of the case. | |
| | | |
| Enfield | Nay, 'tis a phrase most accurate and apt. | |
| | There's aught in his appearance yet unfashion'd, | |
| | Displeasing, verily detestable. | |
| | I never saw a man I so dislik'd, | 95 |
| | Yet scarce can I describe wherefore 'tis so. | |
| | He gives a sense of broad deformity, | |
| | But no distortion of a body part | |

|  | Can I identify, though I have tried— |  |
|---|---|---|
|  | And 'tis not for a want of memory, | 100 |
|  | For troth, my mind's eye sees him even now. |  |
|  | "Extraordinary" is the word exact, |  |
|  | Yet in a manner quite unnamable. |  |

Utterson What is the name of this unsav'ry man?

Enfield One Edward Hyde.

Utterson —E'en he!

Enfield —Dost know the man? 105

Utterson Coincidence ne'er came with more surprise:
That name is at the center of a case
O'er which I would make enquiry anon.
'Twas my intention, following our stroll,
To visit Doctor Lanyon.

Enfield —Lanyon, why? 110

Utterson To ask about the man whose name thou speak'st,
And his association with my client,
One Doctor Henry Jekyll.

Enfield —He it is
Whose name was writ on that bill of exchange!

Utterson What I suspected thou hast now confirm'd. 115
I tell thee this in strictest confidence,
Upon our friendship's many years of trust.

Enfield Thou never shalt have reason, sir, to doubt me.

| | | |
|---|---|---|
| Utterson | 'Twas recently—a fortnight hence, perhaps— | |
| | When Doctor Jekyll came to visit me, | 120 |
| | Announcing that he wish'd to change his will | |
| | And name a newfound beneficiary. | |
| | In case of the decease of Henry Jekyll, | |
| | His every possession should at once | |
| | Become the property and assets of | 125 |
| | His friend and benefactor Edward Hyde. | |
| | | |
| Enfield | The mystery grows deeper, ever deeper. | |
| | | |
| Utterson | There's more: he bid me write that in the case | |
| | That he, himself, should somehow disappear | |
| | Or undergo an absence unexplain'd | 130 |
| | For any period beyond three months, | |
| | This Edward Hyde should step into his shoes | |
| | Without delay, live free from any burden | |
| | Or obligation past the payment of | |
| | A few small sums to Doctor Jekyll's household. | 135 |
| | | |
| Enfield | What could this mean? Hast thou been party to | |
| | Such strange requests from clients in the past? | |
| | | |
| Utterson | Not once. Methought, at first, 'twas madness plain, | |
| | Yet now I start to fear it is disgrace. | |
| | | |
| Enfield | We come e'en now to Doctor Lanyon's home. | 140 |
| | This new development amazeth me— | |
| | Wouldst thou object if I beheld thy conf'rence? | |
| | | |
| Utterson | Nay. Hereupon I name thee my law partner, | |
| | Associate—if junior—on the case. | |
| | | |
| Enfield | Ha! Watch how I do come up in the world, | 145 |
| | And 'tis not lunchtime yet. | |

Utterson                    —Yea. Keep this pace,
                    And thou shalt be a magistrate ere supper.


*They knock on a door. Enter HASTIE LANYON through it.*


Lanyon          Ah, Mister Utterson! My longtime friend,
                    Why dost thou darken doors as low as mine?


Utterson          Good morrow, Lanyon. Know'st thou Richard
                                                            Enfield?   150


Lanyon          By reputation I do know him well,
                    Yet in the flesh far less than I could wish.
                    Ye are both welcome warmly, gentlemen.


Enfield          Good day to you and all health, Doctor Lanyon.


Lanyon          A friend of Utterson's is friend of mine,          155
                    I prithee call me Hastie.


Enfield                    —Right away,
                    And from this moment forward.


Lanyon                    —How have I
                    So pleas'd the gods to earn this visit rare?


Utterson          I'll to the point, that we may not disturb
                    Thy Sunday morning more than is requir'd.       160
                    Wouldst thou agree that thou and I must be
                    The oldest friends that Henry Jekyll hath?


Lanyon          Well could I wish the friends were younger men,
                    But I suppose we are. Yet what of that?
                    I see the man but little recently.              165


24

| | |
|---|---|
| Utterson | Indeed? Methought you two did share a bond |
| | Of common int'rest. |
| | |
| Lanyon | —Yea, but 'tis long past. |
| | Of late, the noble Henry Jekyll hath |
| | Become too fanciful for even me. |
| | Most plainly, he began to go awry: 170 |
| | Most errant, wrong in mind, full of such thoughts— |
| | In truth, unscientific balderdash— |
| | That would have caus'd disunity betwixt |
| | E'en Damon and Phythias, those two friends |
| | Of ancient myth, whose close relationship 175 |
| | Did stay their execution at the hand |
| | Of Dionysius of Syracuse. |
| | |
| Utterson | *[aside:]* Perchance his falling out with Doctor Jekyll |
| | Was o'er some point of scientific thought. |
| | Thank heaven it was such a minor thing. 180 |
| | *[To Lanyon:]* Art thou familiar with one Edward Hyde, |
| | Who is, I gather, Doctor Jekyll's pupil— |
| | An acolyte or follower of his? |
| | |
| Lanyon | Nay, never have I heard the person's name. |
| | |
| Utterson | I thank thee, sir. We'll leave thee to thy rest, 185 |
| | And much I hope we'll have occasion soon |
| | To raise a glass or share a meal as one, |
| | And revel in each other's company. |
| | |
| Enfield | All good health, Hastie. |
| | |
| Lanyon | —God be with you both. |
| | I hope this Sunday taketh ye wheree'er 190 |
| | Your wand'ring spirits long to go. Farewell! |

*[Exit Lanyon into his house.*

| | |
|---|---|
| Enfield | This is most inconclusive. |
| Utterson |     —Verily. |

Enfield     How shalt thou, then, proceed to find the cause
    For Doctor Jekyll's sudden change of mind?

Utterson     Thou hast a keen advantage over me,     195
For thou hast seen the man, this Edward Hyde.
Methinks if I may set mine eyes on him,
The mystery, now shroud in darker hues,
May lighten as the coming of the dawn,
And peradventure disappear completely,     200
As hidden things will do when well-examin'd.
Perhaps, if I behold the man himself,
I may discover rhyme or reason for
Whatever preference or bondage—thou
Mayst choose the phrase—my friend encountereth,   205
Which led unto the startling, baffling clause
Writ into his last will and testament.
By thine admission, Enfield, it at least
Shall be a face worth seeing, such as hath
Prov'd fearful to thine eyes and rais'd in thee     210
A spirit of enduring detestation.

Enfield     Though I would gladly shun the dreadful sight,
It may prove as thou sayest, Utterson.

Utterson     I'll haunt the district of which thou didst speak—
He's Mister Hyde; I shall be Mister Seek.     215

*[Exeunt.*

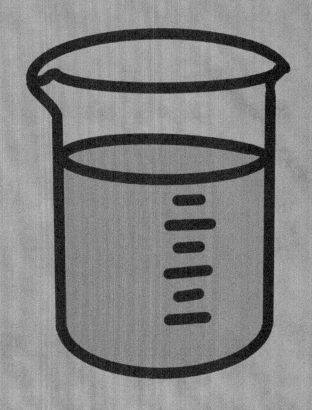

# ACT II

# SCENE 1.

*A street, near a side entrance to Jekyll's residence.*

*Enter EDWARD HYDE, preparing to enter.*

| | | |
|---|---|---|
| Hyde | A pleasant afternoon for deeds most vile, | |
| | For I have wander'd through the city streets | |
| | Engaging in such shameless, bold misdeeds | |
| | That I were soon undone were I found out. | |
| | I tripp'd a monk upon Great Peter Street, | 5 |
| | Set free a carthorse bound on Bridle Lane, | |
| | Stole costly western foxwhelp fruit on Eastcheap, | |
| | And kick'd a vagrant cat on Francis Street. | |
| | Yet these are simple trifles, nothing else, | |
| | And merely stir mine appetite for more— | 10 |
| | To drink of evil doth increase my thirst, | |
| | To feast on sin makes me the hungrier. | |
| | Why set the baser instincts in me free | |
| | If they are never given full expression? | |

*Enter GABRIEL JOHN UTTERSON, unseen.*

| | | |
|---|---|---|
| Utterson | *[aside:]* My many nights of labor, watching for | 15 |
| | Th'appearance of this solitary man | |
| | Have paid their dividends at last—'tis he! | |
| | Or so I feel it must be, for behold, | |
| | The man is small, his moves most serpentine, | |
| | And he doth slither slyly to the door— | 20 |
| | Yet 'tis not that same door which Enfield spake of, | |
| | This is good Doctor Jekyll's residence! | |
| | The door he doth prepare to enter leads | |
| | To Doctor Jekyll's lab'ratory, which | |
| | Connecteth, via hallways, to his home. | 25 |
| | See how this man approacheth confidently, | |
| | As if he were a welcome guest therein, | |

As if the lab'ratory were his own,
As if 'twere natural. I have him now!
Soon all that's cover'd o'er shall be unveil'd,                    30
Soon lawlessness shall answer to the right,
Soon this short swindler shall be known at length.
*[Coming forward:]* Beg pardon—you are Mister Hyde, I
                                                                think?

                    *[Hyde responds but does not face Utterson.*

Hyde            Alack, who cometh on me suddenly?
                Such is my name. What dost thou want of me?        35

Utterson        If I affrighted you, please be at ease:
                I am a friend of Doctor Henry Jekyll—
                One Mister Utterson of Gaunt Street, I—
                And wonder'd, as it seems you're bound inside,
                If you might kindly grant to me admittance.         40

Hyde            Herein thou shalt not Doctor Jekyll find;
                He is from home. How didst thou know my name?

Utterson        Should I respond, may I one favor ask?

Hyde            'Tis not my habit, granting favors odd
                To gentlemen unknown. What shall it be?             45

Utterson        Pray, look on me and let me see your face,
                That, in the future, I'll know you again.

Hyde            *[aside:]* A man most forward and impertinent,
                Would he look on the face of Edward Hyde?
                I'd gladly hide his face with mine own knife.       50
                            *[He turns to Utterson, facing him.*

*[Aloud:]* Now have I shown thee, thou must play thy part:
How didst thou know me?

Utterson           —By description, sir.
'Twas your appearance that reveal'd your name.

Hyde         Nay, more exact thou must be. Whose description?
Who tells a tale of Mister Edward Hyde,       55
How he is, by his stature, recogniz'd,
How his comportment gives away the man,
How one may know him even by his gait,
How doubt shall fall away by how he stands?

Utterson     *[aside:]* It seemeth I have touch'd upon a nerve—    60
The face, as yet unchang'd, starts to transform.
*[Aloud:]* We have, sir, common friends, 'Tis nothing more.

Hyde         Name, then, a single friend whom we do share.

Utterson     Good Doctor Jekyll foremost, by my troth.

Hyde         How goes the world awry when gentleman    65
May block the way of strangers in the street,
Ply them with questions unreservedly,
And crown their errant action with a lie!
Old Jekyll never told thee of me, sir,
On this I'd swear my life unto my death.       70
Thou seekest me, yet 'tis I who did find
Thee in a falsehood, rank and undeserv'd.

Utterson     Come, come, you need not use such language harsh.

Hyde         Is this thine only answer? Get thee gone,
Or gladly shall I hail a constable.          75

*[Hyde exits through the door.*

Utterson        'Tis certain that he caught me in a lie,
Yet there is something more that he conceals.
The man seems hardly human, verily—
More like some bygone ancestor of ours,
Enow alike humanity by sight,          80
Yet with a soul so eminently foul
The human aspect is besmirchèd quite.
Poor Henry—if e'er Satan's signature
Were writ upon a face, 'tis on thy friend,
This Mister Hyde. Thus, for my client and    85
My friend, e'en Jekyll, I shall seek to solve
This myst'ry, come what may. I'll knock again,
Yet not upon the lab'ratory door,
But, like a gentleman, around the front.

*He rounds the corner and knocks on the front door. Enter POOLE.*

Poole        Good even, sir.

Utterson          —Ah, Poole. How pleasant 'tis    90
That thou dost make an answer when I knock,
And no one else. Is Doctor Jekyll home?

Poole        You are most welcome, Mister Utterson.
If you will step inside, I'll search for him.

Utterson        *[stepping in:]* Full thanks, Poole, for thy hospitality.   95

Poole        One moment, sir, and I shall soon discover
If Doctor Jekyll is within the house.

                                        *[Exit Poole.*

Utterson        This man's the picture of civility,
The opposite of vulgar Mister Hyde.

|  | |  |
|---|---|---|
|  | Here is a Poole where one would gladly drink, | 100 |
|  | A Poole that is a fount of courtesy, | |
|  | A Poole wherein a man could swim in peace, | |
|  | A Poole whose waters teem with pleasantries. | |

*Enter POOLE.*

| Poole | Alas, sir, Doctor Jekyll is—*[Aside:]* what word | |
|---|---|---|
|  | May I employ to speak a grain of truth | 105 |
|  | Whilst showing steadfast loyalty unto | |
|  | My worthy master?—*[Aloud:]* absent, verily. | |

| Utterson | 'Tis well, Poole. I shall visit him again. | |
|---|---|---|
|  | One question further: I saw Mister Hyde | |
|  | Make entrance by the lab'ratory door. | 110 |
|  | Is he such access and permission giv'n, | |
|  | E'en when our Doctor Jekyll is from home? | |

| Poole | Quite right—'tis just so, Mister Utterson. | |
|---|---|---|
|  | He hath a key and my kind master's leave. | |

| Utterson | It seems thy master doth repose much trust | 115 |
|---|---|---|
|  | In that young man, Poole. | |

| Poole | —Yea, he doth indeed. | |
|---|---|---|
|  | The staff and I are under orders to | |
|  | Obey the man in ev'ry wish and whim, | |
|  | To treat his biddings as imperatives | |
|  | As if by Doctor Jekyll's own decree. | 120 |

| Utterson | Methinks I ne'er met Mister Hyde on those | |
|---|---|---|
|  | Occasions when I came to dine with Jekyll. | |

| Poole | Nay, sir, the man dines not within the house. | |
|---|---|---|
|  | We see but little of him on this side, | |

               For 'tis his wont to enter by the door            125
               At which you saw him, by the lab'ratory.

**Utterson**       My thanks again, Poole, for thine able help.

**Poole**          Godspeed, sir—may you find what you do seek.

**Utterson**       Good night, Poole.

**Poole**               —Mister Utterson, farewell.

*[Exit Poole.*

**Utterson**       My mind misgives that Jekyll is caught up     130
               In deeper waters, far from Poole's protection.
               'Tis true that Jekyll was a wild young man,
               Perchance some canker of conceal'd disgrace
               Ariseth as a punishment severe,
               For, in the law of God, there's limit none.     135
               'Tis certain that, were Hyde beneath the scope,
               We'd soon discover secrets of his own,
               Dark secrets, judging by his wickèd mien,
               And Jekyll's secrets next to his would shine
               Like morning sun. This must not be allow'd—     140
               This creature shall not steal, like some vile thief,
               The records and the papers Jekyll holds
               And so disrupt the household of my friend.
               If Hyde suspects th'existence of the will,
               He may prove quite impatient to inherit,     145
               And what base deeds might he, then undertake?
               I must see Jekyll, though this rogue beset me,
               And then pursue this case, if he shall let me.

*[Exit.*

## SCENE 2.

*Inside Jekyll's residence.*

*Enter POOLE.*

Poole          Fulfillment of my duties, in the past,
Requireth tact, discretion, and devotion.
My master doth not bear perfection's mark,
Yet is far purer than the common sort,
And, therefore, as his man, it is my duty       5
To keep from him those who do love him not.
I do not hesitate to tell white lies
To guard him from the taint of darker hues.
I do not flinch to risk my character
To make his shine the brighter by the deed.       10
Of late, though, bonds of loyalty are push'd,
Stretch'd thin, abus'd, e'en to the breaking point—
While for my master I'd do anything,
His actions lately pass my comprehension.
Who is this Mister Hyde who, suddenly,       15
Becomes a fixture of the household's days?
Appearing swift as day turns into night—
In nature like a storm to Jekyll's calm,
His aspect foul where Jekyll's is most fair,
His manner rude when Jekyll is refin'd—       20
I never met a man more contrary,
The opposite of Jekyll utterly.
That I should mislead Mister Utterson
Because my master's indispos'd upon
The coming of this Mister Hyde—fie, Poole!       25
This is not servanthood, but servitude,
And doth demand its answer by and by.

*Enter EDWARD HYDE on balcony, in HENRY JEKYLL's chamber,
unseen by POOLE.*

Hyde          Alas, I went abed as Henry Jekyll,

And find myself awake as Edward Hyde.

Bless me, I am translated in my sleep!      30

*[Poole hears him and calls to him.*

Poole         Sir, is that you? Shall I prepare your breakfast?

Hyde          O, Poole! *[Aside:]* Alas, this is not Jekyll's sound.

*[In Jekyll's voice:]* Forgive the untried voice of morning

time,

Which creeps into the throat and croaks like frog.

I speak but nonsense. Breakfast, didst thou say?   35

Yea, e'en as thou proposest shall it be,

Methinks I could a double portion eat,

A feast for two men suited, not just one.

Poole         As is your will, sir. Have you further needs?

Hyde          *[aside:]* I must unto the lab'ratory hie,      40

Yet would not be espied by mine own staff,

Who scurry round the house like daybreak mice,

Or they shall see the little hands of Hyde,

Fit for such deeds as suit a miscreant,

Unlike the large, strong hands of Henry Jekyll.   45

They'll gaze upon the mean and haggard face,

Which frightens rats such that they scamper hence,

Dissimilar in full to Jekyll's visage.

They shall the smaller size of Hyde's frame spy,

Design'd for darting, ducking, taking flight,     50

Distinct from Jekyll's tall and gallant form.

I must take pains that they observe me not.

*[To Poole:]* A dream most scientific have I had,
Of elements and potions and the like,
Which I must put unto the test anon—                         55
Experiments brook no delay.

Poole                    —'Tis well.
You shall be undisturb'd till you emerge.

Hyde          And let the staff not look on me as I
Make way unto my lab'ratory, Poole.

Poole         Not look on you?

Hyde                    —Those were my words exact.          60
A dream's a fragile thing, as thou dost know,
Prone to dissolving like the fog at dawn,
And I suspect that, were I merely glimps'd
By human eyes whilst I but hardly grasp it,
The thought ought turn to naught and be not caught. 65

Poole         You would not have us look on you.

Hyde                    —E'en so.

Poole         I shall instruct the staff t'avert their eyes.

Hyde          Good Poole, thou loyal Poole, thou worthy Poole,
Such Poole as shows reflection of oneself—
Thou show'st both patience and fidelity.                    70

Poole         'Tis but mine honor. When you are yourself—
By which I mean in state of mind to eat,
And finish'd with the morn's experiments—
Your breakfast shall await.

Hyde                  —My many thanks,
But some few minutes and I'll be along.        75

*[Exit Hyde.*

Poole         O, what a noble mind is here o'erthrown—
Are these the ravings of a lunatic
Or trifles of the scientific brain?
The difference is indiscernible,
Which, of itself, is mystery enow.          80
*[A knock is heard at the door.*
Who knocks? Shall I invent excuses further?

*He opens the door. Enter GABRIEL JOHN UTTERSON.*

Utterson      Good morrow, Poole.

Poole              —Ah, Mister Utterson!

Utterson      Like stallion running round enclosèd field,
Another lap I've made and have return'd
To seek my friend, thy master. Is he home?      85

Poole         He is sir, but I fear he's indispos'd—

*Enter HENRY JEKYLL.*

Jekyll         Nay, Poole, I am myself, and fain would I
Give welcome unto Mister Utterson.
*[Aside to Poole:]* My thanks for thy discretion and
                                             support.
Prepare my morning meal, as thou didst proffer.     90

*[Poole nods and exits.*

Utterson         Good morrow, Jekyll. Long I've search'd for thee—
Thou art like mist, e'er vanishing in th'air,
Impossible to gather or contain.

Jekyll         Apologies, old friend. I have, of late,
Been busy with the work of two men.

Utterson                 —Well,        95
Thou art here now, and I'll not keep thee long.
I've wish'd to speak with thee about thy will.

Jekyll         *[aside:]* The very topic which I would avoid.
*[To Utterson:]* Alas, poor Utterson, unfortunate
Art thou in such a client as myself.        100
Ne'er did I see a man so wan with trouble,
So out of joint and rife with fretfulness,
As thou art o'er my will and testament—
Excepting Lanyon, o'er what he doth call
My errant scientific heresies—        105
Yet never mind, I prithee frown thou not,
He is a man most excellent, in troth,
Whom I do ever wish to see the more—
And yet a hide-bound pedant, for all that,
Most ignorant and blatant in his ways,        110
Insufferable in the nits he picks;
Ne'er was I more frustrated by a man.

Utterson        *[aside:]* This tirade over Mister Lanyon is
Both unexpected and unfortunate.
I must but note it and move to the point.        115
*[To Jekyll:]* Thou knowest well I never did approve't.

Jekyll         The will? Forsooth, thou mad'st thy will well known.

Utterson        My will o'er thy will bears a repetition:
                Much have I learned about young Mister Hyde.

Jekyll          If that is the direction thou wouldst take,                    120
                I cannot join thee in the dialogue.
                Thou runnest off with suppositions like
                The hare who looks upon the tortoise slow
                And understandeth not the steady gait,
                Yet in the end doth lose the race entire.                      125
                This matter, sir, is clos'd betwixt we two.

Utterson        Yet what I heard was most abominable.

Jekyll          There's naught can alter what I have decreed.
                Thou canst not my position comprehend—
                'Tis strange, 'tis passing strange, 'tis pitiful,             130
                'Tis wondrous pitiful—and shall not be
                Amended by more talking, Utterson.

Utterson        Thou mayst be certain, Jekyll, of my trust.
                Unburden thyself of this weary load
                By taking me within thy confidence.                           135
                The truth is, there are no friends good or bad:
                Perhaps mere friends, who stand by one when one
                Is hurting, to relieve one's loneliness.
                Perhaps these friends are worth the being scar'd,
                Or hoping for them, living for them, too.                      140
                Perhaps these friends are worth the dying for,
                Should that be where the situation leads.
                No good friends and no bad friends neither, nay:
                But only those one wants and needs to be with,
                Those people who build houses in one's heart.                 145
                I've no doubt I can set you free from this,
                Whatever is the "it" that it may be.

Jekyll        Good Utterson, this speaketh well of thee,
And no words can I find t'express my thanks.
Thy kind assurances I do believe,        150
And I would trust thee ere another man—
Aye, even ere myself, could I but choose—
The case, howe'er, is not as foul as thine
Imagination fruitful fancieth—
Pray, put your noble, caring heart at rest.    155
To set your mind at ease, hear thou these words:
Whenever I desire, I can be rid
Of Mister Hyde. I swear it, on my life.
With that oath, sir, please let the matter sleep:
It is most private, priz'd, and personal.    160

Utterson      Like ship when howling, raging storm doth break,
Thou settest me in calmer waters, Jekyll.

Jekyll        Since we have touch'd upon the subject now—
And for, I hope, the last time—there is one
Point further I'd like thee to understand:    165
I have an int'rest keen in this poor Hyde.
I know thou hast seen him; he told me so,
And, by his telling, I fear he was rude.
Sincerely, though, he is my great concern,
Alike as if he were my other self,    170
And I shall be oblig'd if thou wilt pledge
To bear with him and get his rights for him
Should I be ta'en away. If thou knew'st all,
Methinks thou wouldst not—couldst not—hesitate.
If thou but promise, 'twould reduce the weight    175
Of care and worry on mine anxious mind.

Utterson      I'll not pretend to ever like the man.

| | | |
|---|---|---|
| Jekyll | I ask not liking—only justice, sir— | |
| | To help him, for my sake, if I am gone. | |
| | | |
| Utterson | Thou hast my word, and thus I take my leave. | 180 |
| | | |
| Jekyll | And with thy word, my thanks and fond farewell. | |

*[Exit Utterson.*

How shall I justify, to men as these,
The strange experiments I've underta'en?
Born into wealth, endow'd with ev'ry gain,
Inclin'd by nature unto industry,                    185
Enjoying the respect of humankind,
I'd ev'ry guarantee of honor, fame,
A future most distinguish'd 'mongst the rest.
Yet ne'er could I the darkness reconcile,
Those pleasures I conceal'd as I sought praise.      190
E'en as a young man, I already stood
Committed to duplicity of life.
Mine aspirations and my degradations
Were warring factions in a single breast,
My good and ill were sever'd utterly.                195
As scientific studies I pursued,
Which led to mystic, transcendental thoughts,
I drew more steadily unto the truth,
Discovery of which hath doom'd me to
A dreadful shipwreck on the rocks of fate:           200
We humans are not truly one, but two.
Two, say I, though the truth may lie beyond:
Perchance the denizens within the mind
Are multifarious and independent.
Yet two was plenty for my studies rare,              205
The primitive duality of each,
Two natures in one consciousness oppos'd.
'Twas from an early date I learn'd to dwell
With pleasure—an illuminating daydream—

41

Upon the sev'rance of these elements,                          210
The separation of identities.
Then, peradventure, would our living be
Reliev'd of all the thousand nat'ral shocks—
The whips and scorns of time that all do bear—
Unjustness trav'ling on its evil way,                          215
Uprightness walking on the better path.
Yet, can a person such as Utterson—
Or any noble, simple man like he,
See past the petty fortunes of the world
And understand the value of my work?                           220
Am I abandon'd in the universe,
A voice that crieth in the wilderness
Where none shall hear the truth that I proclaim?
Nay, not alone, not e'er, for this is true:
I am no longer one. With Hyde, I'm two.                        225

                                                        [*Exit.*

## SCENE 3.
### *A street.*

*Enter EDITH, a maidservant, on balcony.*

Edith          From here, above the street, safe in my home,
               The world seems lovely, quiet, and serene.
               How like a painting is the avenue—
               The yellow light doth dapple cobblestones,
               The lane's at rest, done with its daily toil,        5
               Those who traverse it trav'ling home to sleep,
               A fog begins with little wisps and whispers,
               The moon above shines brightly o'er the scene.
               Methinks I ne'er was more at perfect peace
               With all humanity as I am now,                      10

42

Or thought more kindly of my fellow folk
As I do, gazing o'er the tranquil road.

*Enter EDWARD HYDE with a walking stick, below.*

| | | |
|---|---|---|
| Hyde | For many weeks have I been bound within, | |
| | And with such throes and longings struggl'd for | |
| | My freedom, till old Jekyll did release me. | 15 |
| | Behold the vast occasions, now, for vice. | |

Edith       Behold the little man down in the street—
'Tis Mister Edward Hyde, whom I have seen
Once visiting my kindly master's house.
Then did I look on him with some dislike,    20
Yet must my intuition overcome.
How sweet he seems now, like a gentle sprite.

Hyde      How full of vice I seem, e'en like a drunkard
Who's not affected by the dangers of
His physical insensibility.    25
Yea, Jekyll made allowance far too small
For my insensate readiness to sin.
The devil, too long cag'd, hath been set free,
Now shall he come out roaring through the night.

Edith      Now shall he make way softly through the night.    30

*Enter DANVERS CAREW below, encountering HYDE.*
*EDITH watches them.*

Carew      Good even, sir, and safest travels home.

Edith      A chance encounter in the midnight air—
Perchance these strangers two shall turn fast friends
Amongst the peaceable and soothing haze.

Hyde   Thou fool, pray get thee from my presence, lest  35
      My feral spirit hath its way with thee.
      *[Aside:]* A tempest of impatience grows within,
      A furious propensity to ill
      That boils my blood at his civilities.

Carew   Excuse me! Such an insult is unjust,   40
      And you, sir, have no cause to use me so.
      I am a member of our parliament,
      A gentleman of reputation spotless.
      Apologize at once for your rash words.

Hyde   Wouldst thou have some confession of regret?  45

Carew   Such is the recompense that I am ow'd.

Hyde   I'll give thee what I owe thee, verily.

           *[Hyde begins to beat Carew with the stick.*

Edith   Fie, Hyde attacks! No merry meeting this!
      Alas, his viciousness doth break the peace
      That otherwise had o'er the nighttime reign'd.  50
      I am grown watchful by this great attack!

Hyde   I am grown weary of thy little life,
      Like angry child who, midst a tantrum wild,
      Destroys the trinkets that delight him not,
      Turns playthings into nothings in a trice!  55

Carew   O, yet defend me, someone; I'm but hurt!

            *[Hyde continues beating Carew.*

Edith        The sounds of twisting limbs and breaking bones
Reach even from below unto mine ears,
Where like a club they do assault my mind.
O horror, horror passing all belief!        60

*[She faints.*

Hyde        O pleasure, pleasure passing ev'ry doubt!
No instincts balancing are mine tonight—
No gentleness to curb my forcefulness,
No sympathy to tame brutality,
No introversion silencing perversion,        65
No common sense to o'ercome violence.
Temptation unto murder hath its sway
And overtaketh me deliciously.
Yea, ev'ry blow is color'd with delight,
I gladly maul his unresisting frame,        70
A thrill of terror aiming at my heart.

*[Carew dies.*

The deed is done, his life made forfeit now—
Yet mine as well, unless I fly anon.
Unto my house, where I shall soon destroy
The papers—they, the record of my days—        75
Such evidence as might my guilt ensure.
What actions wonderful I've done this night!

*[Exit Hyde. Edith awakes.*

Edith        What visions horrible I've seen this night!
How might I wish that I—awaking here—
Might, as from nightmare, realize what I saw        80
Was but a harmless drama of the mind.
Yet, looking at the avenue below,
I see the truth as clear as words on page:
The body of a man unmoving, crush'd,

Death's final promise on the tortur'd face.                    85
Am I the only witness to this crime?
Then, Edith, use thy voice and tell the world.
*[Calling out the window:]* Help, ho! Foul murder!
                                   Murder in our streets!

Enter *INSPECTOR NEWCOMEN.*

Newcomen     Who calls? Of late was I on my patrol,
             And heard thy cries. Dost speak of murder, miss?    90

Edith        The foulest sort—behold the body there.
             Give me a moment, and I shall descend.

                                          *[Exit Edith.*

Newcomen     Alas, a victim even as she saith,
             Whose body tells the story of its death.
             How mangl'd is the corse, how bent the frame!    95
             This stick, with which the evil deed was done—
             Composèd of a rare, tough, heavy wood—
             Lies partly splinter'd on the avenue.
             It must have shatter'd underneath the load
             Of vicious and uncaring cruelty.                 100
             Belike the murderer hath carried hence
             The other portion of this selfsame stick,
             Which may yet be a clue for their arrest.
             A purse, a gold watch, both were left behind,
             Suggesting motive more than robbery.             105
             There are no cards and papers on the man,
             Except—what's this?—a sealèd envelope,
             Which bears the name of Gabriel Utterson,
             A local lawyer of a good repute.

*Enter EDITH.*

| | | |
|---|---|---|
| Edith | I thank you, sir, for coming urgently. | 110 |
| | How can I help, Inspector— | |
| | | |
| Newcomen | —Newcomen. | |
| | Dost thou know Gabriel Utterson? | |
| | | |
| Edith | —The lawyer? | |
| | I know of him, but not the man himself. | |
| | | |
| Newcomen | He lives nearby. | |
| | | |
| Edith | —Indeed, I know the place. | |
| | | |
| Newcomen | Pray, go and fetch him— | |
| | | |
| Edith | —Edith— | |
| | | |
| Newcomen | —Edith, lass. | 115 |
| | This case shall have much need of him anon. | |
| | | |
| Edith | Say he is not suspected of the crime, | |
| | For I believe I saw the man at fault. | |
| | | |
| Newcomen | More shall we speak of that in time, my lady. | |
| | | |
| Edith | I shall return with Mister Utterson. | 120 |

*[Exit Edith.*

| | |
|---|---|
| Newcomen | A troubl'd city London hath become, |
| | With crime in ev'ry neighborhood and port. |
| | 'Twas last October, on All-Hallows' Eve, |
| | A lad named Michael slew his sister pure, |

Was apprehended by constabularies,                    125
And now is one of Bedlam's residents,
Where Doctor Loomis doth observe the boy.
Meanwhile, near Crystal Palace, there have been
Reports of many youths who have been slain
By monster rising from the wat'ry depths.              130
One Madam Voorhees was our only lead,
Yet then the woman was beheaded found.
And strangest, possibly, of all these crimes
Is Elm Street, site of last year's schoolhouse fire,
Where multiple accounts speak of a rogue              135
Who slaughters people whilst in slumber deep,
And goeth by the name of Frederick.
Such horrible events as none would credit—
This is what London sadly hath become;
Policemen's lot is not a happy one.                   140

*Enter EDITH and GABRIEL JOHN UTTERSON.*

Edith          Good Mister Utterson arriveth, sir.

Utterson       The lady hath describ'd what did befall,
               The senseless beating of a blameless man.

Newcomen       I give thee thanks for stirring from thy home
               And coming quickly.

Utterson                    —When I heard the news,         145
               No thought of rest or slumber could I have.
               I recognize the face of this poor man,
               Who lies so beaten and so broken here:
               I'll wager this is Danvers—Sir Carew.

Newcomen       Good god! Carew of parliament?

| | | |
|---|---|---|
| Utterson | —E'en he. | 150 |

Newcomen   This shall a most upsetting story make,
One that shall echo widely through the town.

Edith   Methinks I knew the man who did the deed?

Newcomen   Who was the villain?

Edith   —Mister Edward Hyde.

Utterson   *[aside:]* Such was my fear, but hop'd 'twould not be
so.   155

Newcomen   I do not know the man. Yet, Utterson,
By how thy mien turns paler than the moon,
It seemeth thou dost know of whom she speaks?

Utterson   I have, unhapp'ly, met the horrid man.

Newcomen   Behold the murder weapon, this large stick—   160

Utterson   How terror follows terror sans relief!

Newcomen   Know'st thou this wood as well? To know a man
Is commonplace; acquaintance with a stick
Bespeaks intelligence unusual.

Utterson   That same stick I presented years ago   165
To Doctor Henry Jekyll. O, good Henry,
What tangl'd webs art thou ensnar'd within,
Where spiders slink about to wrap thee tight
And suck the very lifeblood out of thee?
I bid thee, Edith, art thou sure 'twas Hyde?   170
Didst thou behold the stature of the man?

| | |
|---|---|
| Edith | Particularly small and wickèd-looking, |
| | Yea, short of form yet powerful enow |
| | To beat this sorry man unto the death. |

Utterson      The portrait thou dost paint is apt: 'twas Hyde.     175

Newcomen     Dost know where we can find the criminal?

Utterson      Tonight, perchance, to justice he'll be brought—
                 I'll take thee to his house immediately.
                 Come, let us forward with one mind, inspector,
                 Soon shall we exorcise the vicious specter.     180

*[Exeunt.*

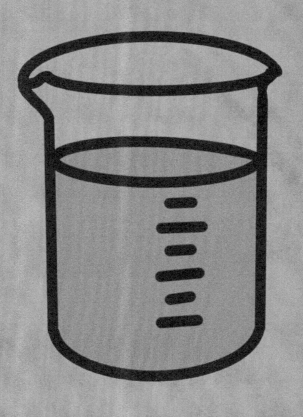

# ACT III

## SCENE 1.

*Hyde's residence.*

*Enter RUTH.*

Ruth  A dreadful night, with omens menacing—
     The moon is in its fullness in the sky,
     And in the distance there's a wolf that calls
     With howls of sharpest woe and direst threat.
     The resident—I do not call him master—    5
     Who dwells within this house is come and gone
     Like hurricane that maketh landfall sudden
     And blows once more to sea, more havoc wreaking.

*A knock at the door. RUTH answers. Enter GABRIEL JOHN UTTERSON and INSPECTOR NEWCOMEN.*

Utterson  Ruth! Is it thee?

Ruth     —Yea, Mister Utterson.

Utterson  Yet art thou not of Doctor Jekyll's staff?    10

Ruth    Indeed, sir, but the doctor bid me—

Utterson    —Wait—
     Methinks I can predict what thou shalt say:
     He bid thee be a waiting-woman for
     One Mister Hyde, so precious unto Jekyll.
     Thy services are, as it were, on loan.    15

Ruth    In ev'ry detail you, sir, are correct.

Utterson  Poor Ruth, that thou art bound within this net,
     Which hath been thrown o'er all of London and

Ensnares the city wholly in its cords.
Is Mister Hyde at home?

Ruth                 —He's here and gone.       20
Arriv'd he home past midnight, stay'd not e'en
An hour ere he did venture forth again,
Yet was a tempest of activity.
This, Mister Utterson, was nothing strange.
His habits are beyond irregular—       25
Oft is he absent from this little house.
Ere yesterday he was not seen for weeks.

Utterson     I prithee, Ruth, may we inspect his chamber?

Ruth           Despite my reservations o'er the man,
What manner of housekeeper would I be     30
Should I give my consent unto this search?
My duty makes the task impossible.

Utterson     Thou dost thy office fairly. This man, Ruth,
Is Newcomen of the constabulary.

Ruth           This visit is official, then?

Newcomen      —Quite so.       35

Ruth           And Mister Hyde is in some trouble?

Newcomen      —Yea.

Ruth           My obligation alters at the word.

Newcomen    I'll warrant thou shalt let us search his rooms?

Ruth           Your will is all the warrant I desire.

*[They begin searching.*

| | | |
|---|---|---|
| Utterson | The rooms are fix'd with luxury and taste, | 40 |
| | A closet fill'd with wine, the plate of silver, | |
| | The napery is elegant enow, | |
| | The carpets of good hue and quality. | |
| | Whate'er mine expectation, 'twas not this; | |
| | The house denotes a gentleman refin'd. | 45 |

Newcomen    Come hither, sir! I've found what he was at—
The deeds he plied whilst briefly he was here.
Like smear of sugar on a schoolchild's face
That tells the truth of a forbidden treat,
These ashes on the hearth, still warm by touch,    50
Tell of the papers that were lately burnt.

Utterson    Astounding, Newcomen, and there is more—
Behind this door, behold the second half
Of that ignoble instrument of death:
The selfsame stick that murder'd Sir Carew.    55

Newcomen    We have him! Witness these bills of exchange—
He tried to burn them, too, yet they in part
Surviv'd the conflagration in his haste.
No doubt the man doth safeguard all his money
Within the vaults of one of London's banks.    60
Depend upon it, sir, he's in my grasp:
He must have lost his head, or ne'er would he
Leave stick and bills for our discovery.
He leaves himself completely vulnerable,
As if he'd handed us his very self,    65
For money is the lifeblood of a man.
We've naught to do but wait for him t'appear
Attempting a withdrawal from the bank,
And we shall take him, most assuredly.

| | | |
|---|---|---|
| Utterson | Bold Newcomen, good Ruth, I thank ye for | 70 |
| | Your troubles in pursuit of justice's name. | |
| | | |
| Ruth | No trouble, but a joy to serve the law. | |
| | | |
| Utterson | The morning doth approach—night turns to day— | |
| | I shall to Jekyll and describe the whole. | |
| | This Mister Hyde he can, no more, defend. | 75 |
| | The reign of terror's nearly at an end. | |

*[Exeunt.*

## SCENE 2.
*Jekyll's residence.*

*Enter EDWARD HYDE outside the door to the laboratory.*

| | | |
|---|---|---|
| Hyde | *[sings:]* I sing a song of old Carew, | |
| | The man whom I most gladly slew, | |
| | My actions do not misconstrue, | |
| |    Hey nonny non, the man is gone. | |
| | Although they shall make much ado, | 5 |
| | He'll not be miss'd, this much is true, | |
| | The man was foppish, pompous too, | |
| |    Hey nonny non, 'tis well he's gone. | |
| | Alas, my nighttime spree is through | |
| | And Jekyll must come back in view, | 10 |
| | Or I shall earn a killer's due. | |
| |    Hey nonny non, I must be gone. | |

*[He exits into the laboratory.*

*Enter POOLE and GABRIEL JOHN UTTERSON.*

| | |
|---|---|
| Poole | My master is expected presently— |
| | Methinks I heard him in the lab'ratory. |

| | | |
|---|---|---|
| Utterson | All thanks for granting me admittance, Poole. | 15 |
| | I hope my presence shall not be a shock— | |
| | An unexpected guest may be unwelcome. | |
| | Is it his wont, just after crow of cock, | |
| | To be already in the lab'ratory? | |

| | | |
|---|---|---|
| Poole | 'Tis not unusual; of late it seems | 20 |
| | He spendeth ev'ry waking hour therein. | |

*Enter HENRY JEKYLL.*

| | |
|---|---|
| Jekyll | O Utterson! Art thou come to my home? |

| | | |
|---|---|---|
| Utterson | Dear Henry, thine appearance doth surprise— | |
| | How haggard, pale, and sickly dost thou look, | |
| | As if thou were most ill, e'en unto death. | 25 |

| | |
|---|---|
| Jekyll | Beg pardon, Gabriel, for my morning face. |
| | Were thy call more expected, less surprise, |
| | I should have been a little more myself |
| | And shown to thee a visage more familiar. |
| | Pray, Poole, leave us to speak. |

| | | |
|---|---|---|
| Poole | —As you desire. | 30 |

*[Exit Poole.*

| | |
|---|---|
| Utterson | Hast heard the news? |

| | |
|---|---|
| Jekyll | —They shout it in the square. |

56

'Tis near impossible it should escape
My hearing, even in my dining room.

Utterson    *[aside:]* Though, by the word of Poole, thou camest from
The lab'ratory, not the dining room.                          35
*[Aloud:]* Carew and thou are both my clients, Henry,
And therefore with discretion I'll proceed.
Tell me, I beg, thou hast not reason lost
Such that thou, even now, dost hide the man?
Thou must not seek his safety anymore,                        40
Thou must be sensible of what he's done,
Thou must perceive his guilt and viciousness,
Thou must protection seek from him, not for him.

Jekyll      By heav'n I swear I'll ne'er set eyes on him,
I'm finish'd with the villain in this world.                  45
All's at an end. He seeketh not my help,
And though the man is safe, I promise thee
Thou nevermore shalt hear of him again.

Utterson    How do I hope thy promises prove true.
If e'er this matter unto trial came,                          50
Thy name might, in the whirlwind, be caught up.

Jekyll      I am most sure of him; my certitude
Shall not be buffeted by rumor's storms.
One thing remains, on which thou mayst advise:
A letter have I recently receiv'd,                            55
Which I would have thee read and tell me if
'Tis best to render it to the police.

Utterson    Think'st thou it may unto Hyde's capture lead?

Jekyll      Nay. As Achilles when he would not fight—
Refusing Agamemnon's bold decrees                             60

Although his fellow Greeks were perishing—
My mind is turn'd against the horrid man.
I care not what becomes of Mister Hyde.
'Tis mine own character o'er which I ponder,
Which this foul business hath, I fear, expos'd.                    65

Utterson      *[aside:]* I am surpris'd to see his selfishness,
And yet reliev'd to hear him done with Hyde.
*[Aloud:]* I prithee, Henry, let me see the letter.
                                        *[Jekyll gives Utterson the letter.*
*[Reads:]* "To whomsoever readeth these, my words,
My benefactor, Doctor Henry Jekyll,                               70
Hath too long been unworthily repaid
For his abundant generosities
By me, myself, a scoundrel and a knave.
No soul alive need fear, for I am safe,
With means of sure, dependable escape.                            75
Forgive poor Henry his association
With one who's still an unrepentant sinner:
E'en me who writes this letter, Edward Hyde."
*[To Jekyll:]* The letter is conclusive utterly.
I'll warrant it absolves thee of all fault.                       80
If thou art willing, I shall keep the note,
Bethinking o'er how it portrayeth thee
And whether it should go to the police.

Jekyll        Be thou the judge entirely, Utterson;
All confidence I've lost in mine own self.                        85

Utterson      One question further, ere I take my leave:
Was it this Hyde who dictated the terms
About thy disappearance in the will—
That, if thou suddenly should vanish, he
Would thereupon be heir to thy vast fortune?                      90

| | |
|---|---|
| Jekyll | 'Twas by his will my will was alter'd thus. |
| | |
| Utterson | So I suspected. Hyde intended harm— |
| | He would have murder'd thee and taken all. |
| | Thou hast achiev'd a fortunate escape. |

| | | |
|---|---|---|
| Jekyll | E'en more than an escape, a lesson learn'd— | 95 |
| | Not Icarus, who tried to fly but fell, | |
| | Neither Prometheus, whose fire burn'd him, | |
| | Nor Oedipus, who lov'd where he should not, | |
| | Did learn a harsher lesson than myself. | |

| | | |
|---|---|---|
| Utterson | Farewell until we meet in calmer times. | 100 |

| | |
|---|---|
| Jekyll | For standing with me, Utterson, my thanks. |
| | Thou art both friend and lawyer unto me— |
| | A double nature in a single man. |

*[Exit Jekyll. Utterson leaves by the door and steps into the street.*

| | | |
|---|---|---|
| Utterson | E'en now, I hear the shouts of messengers | |
| | Who tell the news of murder in the streets— | 105 |
| | The death of one who serv'd in parliament. | |
| | Let Hyde's foul name be bound up in the deed | |
| | That my poor friend remaineth shelter'd from | |
| | The crushing Scylla of the present crime | |
| | And swift Charybdis of the scandal's wake. | 110 |
| | To trade an errant knave for noble man | |
| | Is neither sacrifice nor e'en a choice— | |
| | For who among us otherwise would choose? | |

*Enter GUEST, a clerk.*

| | |
|---|---|
| Guest | Good morning, Mister Utterson. |

| | |
|---|---|
| Utterson |    —Ho, Guest. |
| | How comes it that you pass this door e'en now?  115 |
| | |
| Guest | Upon my way to our shar'd office, sir, |
| | For 'tis the morning and the law doth call. |
| | |
| Utterson | Thou art most fortunately met, in troth. |
| | |
| Guest | Am I? |
| | |
| Utterson |    —Thy services and thy keen eyes |
| | Upon the instant would I call upon.  120 |
| | |
| Guest | I am, sir, at your service utterly— |
| | There ne'er was clerk more ready to assist. |
| | |
| Utterson | The news of poor Sir Danvers is most foul. |
| | |
| Guest | Indeed, and public feeling is arous'd, |
| | For ev'rywhere, like fire in tall, dry grass,  125 |
| | The news about it spreadeth speedily. |
| | The man who did the deed, of course, is mad. |
| | |
| Utterson | More of thy views thereon I'd gladly hear. |
| | A letter have I, in his handwriting— |
| |      *[Utterson pulls out the letter.* |
| | Betwixt ourselves this matter must remain,  130 |
| | For scarce know I how matters so complex |
| | Should be administer'd. Still, Guest, behold: |
| | The signature of Hyde, a murderer. |

         *[Guest scans the letter.*

Guest    An odd hand, by my troth. Familiar, too,
       In all my studying of script and letters—    135
       Which, laboring o'er laws and documents,
       Much have I had occasion to pursue—
       Some aspects of this printing have I seen.
       I bid you, have you any specimens
       Of Doctor Henry Jekyll's writing, sir?    140

Utterson   That I should carry such a sample on
       My person were incredible, and yet
       It happens that my pocket doth contain
       An invitation unto dinner writ
       In Jekyll's hand, from many weeks ago.    145

     *[Utterson produces the invitation and hands it to Guest.*

Guest    It shall serve perfectly. One moment, sir.
                *[Guest compares the documents.*
       An interesting autograph, in sooth.

Utterson   Why makest thou compare betwixt the papers?

Guest    The letters bear resemblance singular:
       In many points they are identical—    150
       The slope alone doth set the two apart.
       Were I a mother and these two my babes,
       Belike I would confuse them for each other.

Utterson   Most curious.

Guest       —Forsooth, most curious.

Utterson   This, as thou knowest, Guest, is delicate—    155
       Pray speak not of what thou hast seen today.

Guest    I wholly understand and shall comply.
      Farewell, sir. Shall I see you at the office?

Utterson   Soon shall I be along. I thank thee, Guest.

*[Exit Utterson.*

Guest    Such strange proceedings after such a crime,  160
      Yet these two scripts could not be more alike.
      Is homicide in league with counterfeit?
      Is Jekyll forging for a murderer?
      The once unspeakable seems possible—
      The brink of right and wrong now crossable.  165

*[Exit.*

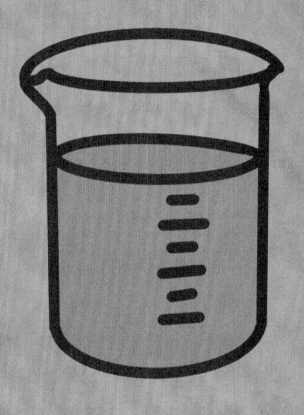

# ACT IV

# SCENE 1.
### *Jekyll's residence.*

*Enter GABRIEL JOHN UTTERSON as Chorus.*

| Utterson | Admit me Chorus to this history | |
|---|---|---|
| | As I, again, relate the story true. | |
| | Once Sir Carew was murder'd, time ran on: | |
| | Though scores of pounds were offer'd in reward— | |
| | For Danvers' death was public injury— | 5 |
| | Sly Mister Hyde had fully disappear'd. | |
| | Tales of his villainy anon were rife; | |
| | From ev'ry corner of the city streets | |
| | Rose confirmations of his cruelty, | |
| | His living vile, his strange associates, | 10 |
| | The hatred which was ever his career. | |
| | Yet now the man was gone, like thunder crash | |
| | That interrupts the stillness of the day | |
| | But then is heard no more. I reckon'd that | |
| | The death of Danvers was repaid in full | 15 |
| | By the departure of rank Mister Hyde. | |
| | New life began for Doctor Jekyll, too, | |
| | Who—like the daffodils that burst through soil | |
| | And welcome spring with promise and delight— | |
| | Came out of his seclusion, saw his friends, | 20 |
| | Once more did entertain as was his wont, | |
| | Was known for charity and righteousness, | |
| | And found, for some two months, his peace again. | |
| | Though none did lay the crime at Jekyll's feet, | |
| | Still, Henry seem'd to say, through deeds, he hop'd | 25 |
| | His future conduct could redeem the past. | |
| | The calm, however, could not last fore'er, | |
| | For Doctor Lanyon—he whom I did visit | |
| | With Enfield after Hyde tromp'd that poor lass— | |
| | This Lanyon did receive a troubling letter, | 30 |
| | The strange beginning of our tragic end. | |

*[Exit.*

*Enter HASTIE LANYON, holding a letter.*

Lanyon           Were more upsetting tidings ever brought
                  Than what a messenger hath just giv'n me?
                  A letter of peculiar quality
                  As I have never read in all my days.         35
                  Alas, I fear my colleague grows insane,
                  When I behold the madman's words he writes.
                  I'll read it o'er again; I must be sure.
                  *[Reads:]* "To Lanyon, thou among my oldest friends:
                  Though we, from time to time have disagreed    40
                  On questions scientific, I believe
                  There is no break in our affection mutual."
                  *[Aside:]* The words thus far are accurate enow—
                  No feelings ill bear I to Henry Jekyll.
                  *[Reads:]* "I would do much for thee, as thou wouldst me. 45
                  Belike thou thinkest, by this overture,
                  The music of my plea shall shameful be—
                  Such must thou judge hereafter for thyself."
                  *[Aside:]* That's an ill phrase, a vile phrase: "judge hereafter."
                  *[Reads:]* "I beg thee stall all thine events tonight,    50
                  E'en if an emperor should summon thee,
                  And hie thee to my house on Hermes' feet.
                  Poole and a locksmith both shall meet thee there:
                  Go quickly to my cabinet, wherein
                  My many papers—all my secrets—dwell,      55
                  And force it ope by any means ye must.
                  Therein shalt thou discover items three,
                  The sum of mine experiments to date:
                  A vial, various powders, and a book.
                  Pray, take them home exactly as they are."     60
                  *[Aside:]* Were this alone the subject of his note,
                  'Twere plenty to astound me to my core,
                  Yet he continues with his bold request.
                  *[Reads:]* "Such is the first of favors two I'll ask.
                  The second, then, is this: when midnight tolls,    65
                  A man will come, presented in my name.
                  Place in his hands the contents—even those
                  That from my cabinet thou didst convey.
                  Then thy role in this drama is fulfill'd,

And thou shalt earn my gratitude complete." 70
*[Aside:]* Who is this man who shall at midnight come?
Were ever more peculiar orders giv'n?
Was e'er a summons curious as this?
Yet this doth he address as he writes on.
*[Reads:]* "When I consider thou mayst not respond— 75
May look upon my bidding as a trifle—
My heart doth sink and hands do tremble so.
Imagine me, I pray, as this is writ,
Hard press'd and weary even unto death,
Beyond what fancy can exaggerate, 80
And knowing that, if thou wilt serve me once,
My troubles roll away like stone from grave,
Wherein lies hope of resurrected life.
Pray serve thy old, dear friend, e'en Henry Jekyll."
*[Aside:]* There ends his letter, and my duty starts. 85
This message I but little understand,
And therefore cannot judge its consequence—
'Tis my responsibility to act.
I therefore have arriv'd at Henry's home,
Responding to his most confusing call. 90

*He knocks on the door. Enter POOLE and a LOCKSMITH.*

Poole          Good evening, Doctor Lanyon.

Lanyon                    —Holla, Poole.
               Belike thou art expecting my arrival?

Poole          Indeed, sir. From my master I receiv'd
               A letter of instruction telling me
               That you would, peradventure, come tonight 95
               And I should call a locksmith—

Locksmith              —He am I!

Poole          To ope my master's cabinet.

Locksmith              —Ho ho!

Lanyon        Thou hast not, then, seen Jekyll recently?

Poole         Not for some seven days now.

Lanyon             —Stranger still.
                 The same entreaty did he make of me,       100
                 Thus have I come.

Poole             —Then let us to it.

Locksmith        —Ha!
                 No lock can long withstand mine instruments.

Poole         But Doctor Lanyon, I forget myself:
                 May I provide aught for your comfort, sir?
                 A drink or some small victuals, possibly?     105

Lanyon         Thou art e'er loyal and hospitable.
                 I thank thee, Poole, yet nothing do require.
                 Let us unto the task we have been left.

Locksmith        Pray, let me at it.

Poole             —Here's the cabinet.
                 Lock'd like the gates of Troy against assault.   110

Locksmith        I'll be a horse and charge with picks and sticks.

Poole         Methinks thou dost not know thy Homer, sir.

Locksmith        At home or not, no lock by human made
                 Can stop the onslaught of a smith like me.
                 I'll warrant I shall have it swiftly op'd.     115

Lanyon         More matter, with less art.

Locksmith             —Unto it, then.
                         *[The locksmith works to open the lock.*
                 Your locks are like your people, by my troth:
                 Some are unmov'd until you find a way

To fill the hole within their inner self,
Some spend their days on pins and needles and 120
Await the perfect match to move their souls,
Some are but lumpish, thick, and plodding bolts,
Which may unlockèd be e'en by a child.
Enow of that, then: you good gods, make me
The penitent instrument to pick this bolt. 125

Lanyon     *[aside to Poole:]* Ne'er knew I locksmith turn'd
                                                    philosopher.

Poole      *[aside to Lanyon:]* In sooth, he oils the latch with slipp'ry
                                                    speech.

                                        *[The cabinet opens.*

Locksmith  Ha! Pegasus hath flown through Ilium's gates
           With good Ajaxes on its worthy back!

Poole      One day, I must regale thee with the story 130
           Of how the Greeks made entry in Troy,
           That thou mayst learn to tell the tale aright.
           But, presently, I'll give thee no correction—
           By heaven, thou art skill'd in smithing locks!

Lanyon     Well done! Methought belike 'twould never ope. 135

Locksmith  'Twas, sir, as easy as when Percules
           Slew Hector on the field at Ithacus.

Poole      Here, Doctor Lanyon, are the papers and
           The vials that my master bid you take.

Lanyon     My thanks, Poole, for thine aid with this strange
                                                    favor. 140
           And thou, too, for the picking of the lock.
           *[Aside:]* I'll hie me home anon, and there await
           Th'arrival of the man of mystery.

                                        *[Exit Lanyon.*

68

| | |
|---|---|
| Poole | If thou art willing and dost have the time, |
| | Perchance a dram of mead thou wouldst enjoy    145 |
| | As I tell thee the stories of old Troy? |
| | |
| Locksmith | Much pleasure take I in thy offer, sir, |
| | And shall enjoy the tales of Agamellon, |
| | Odypheus, Patrinkus, and the rest. |
| | |
| Poole | In Troy, there lies the scene. From isles of Greece   150 |
| | The princes orgulous, their high blood chaf'd, |
| | Have to the port of Athens sent their ships. |
| | |
| Locksmith | Such wondrous words, and from such lavish lips! |

*[Exeunt.*

## SCENE 2.
### *A street, and Lanyon's residence.*

*Enter EDWARD HYDE and a DRIVER in a carriage.*

| | |
|---|---|
| Driver | Good sir, already with a wand'rer's sense |
| | Have we travers'd the city, end to end. |
| | My horses weary grow from all their toil. |
| | Pray, let our journeying concluded be. |
| | |
| Hyde | We have not heard the chimes at midnight yet.    5 |
| | So we must onward till th'appointed time. |
| | A rash of inhumanity doth rise |
| | Within my soul, which shall not let me rest. |

*Enter FLOWER SELLER.*

| | |
|---|---|
| Seller | Well met beneath the stars, kind gentlemen. |
| | Some flowers few my basket still contains—   10 |
| | Would ye care for a bud ere morning comes? |

*[Hyde gets down from the carriage and approaches the flower seller.*

Hyde        Hast thou e'er dancèd with the devil by
The pale moonlight?

Seller             —What means these cryptic words?

Hyde        But this: unless thou wouldst encounter horns,
Thou shouldst not make approach unto the devil.     15
*[Hyde hits the flower seller.*
Now get thee gone!

Seller             —Alack, what have I done
That hath deserv'd such weeds and worms and frost?

*[Exit flower seller, running away.*

Driver       Rogue, thy behavior passeth ev'ry bound
Of courtesy and good society.
Thou mayst no longer in my carriage ride,        20
For thy comportment hath astounded me.

Hyde        If thou declin'st me, sirrah, it shall be
The final words thou ever utterest.
Think carefully, I pray, o'er thy next words.

Driver       *[aside:]* How have I, suddenly, to Charon turn'd,    25
That I should travel to the gates of hell?
Angels and ministers of grace defend me!
*[To Hyde:]* Come, sir, and we shall soon be on our way.

Hyde        Thou findest wisdom, as I knew thou wouldst.

*[Hyde climbs into the carriage. Exeunt.*

*Enter HASTIE LANYON, in his home.*

Lanyon     The articles from Jekyll's cabinets            30
Have I herein examin'd thoroughly.
The powders are a mixture of his own—
They lack th'apothecary's tidy touch,
Though they are neat enow for scientists—

And they appear like salt, of crystals white.     35
The vial, half-full with a red liqueur,
Is highly pungent to the sense of smell,
Belike containing phosphorus and ether,
And looks like naught so much as human blood.
The various ingredients therein     40
I could not guess. Thus, turning to the papers,
There is a book with dates sequential writ,
Which cover many months but comments few:
By some he writeth "Double" and, at first,
There is an entry mark'd as "Total failure."     45
These are but shadows of a hidden truth,
Still too indefinite to see aright.
How might these contents bear upon the life,
The honor, e'en the sanity of Jekyll?
And wherefore shall a messenger arrive     50
And Jekyll not come hither for himself?
These questions have no answers I can find.
Belike the wretchèd man is suffering
From some contamination of the brain.
    *[Lanyon's clock strikes midnight.*
Now midnight strikes, and phantoms may appear.     55

*Enter EDWARD HYDE, knocking at the door. LANYON opens to him.*

Thou are a messenger most punctual,
And com'st from Doctor Jekyll, I presume?

Hyde     Yea.

Lanyon     *[aside:]* —Small is he, but passing muscular,
His garb outsizèd for his little frame.
Th'expression of his face astonishes,     60
Like fish who finds itself on choking land,
Or bat surprisèd by the light of day—
A man torn from his nat'ral element.

Hyde     Dost have the thing for which I travel'd here?

| | | |
|---|---|---|
| Lanyon | Come, sir, I've not made thine acquaintance yet. | 65 |
| | Be seated, prithee, and we two shall speak. | |

Hyde    Beg pardon, Doctor Lanyon. Thou art right;
        Troth, mine impatience stunteth my politeness.
        Methinks thou know'st the urging of thy colleague—
        E'en Doctor Henry Jekyll—brings me here          70
        Upon an enterprise of pith and moment
        To find the contents of a cabinet.

Lanyon  *[pointing:]* There they abideth, e'en as they were found.
                    *[Hyde runs to the contents of the cabinet.*
        *[Aside:]* With cheetah's speed and cunning doth he
                                              pounce!
        I would not be a shrew beneath those claws.        75

Hyde    O marvelous!

Lanyon              —Pray sir, compose thyself.

Hyde    Hast thou a flagon I may briefly use?

*[Lanyon hands him a glass. Hyde mixes the powders and the liquid in the vial.*

Lanyon  *[aside:]* With scientific skill his fingers move,
        As one who hath this tincture mix'd afore.
        How strange for one, appearing as he doth—         80
        Half-craz'd, dishevel'd, wayward, and unruly,
        Like orchard after windstorm passes through—
        To show such technical dexterity.

Hyde    A reddish hue that turns to violet,
        Relaxing unto wat'ry green at last.                85
        The metamorphosis is now complete,
        And thus to settle what remaineth, sir.
        Wilt thou be wise and guided by my will,
        Allowing me to take this chalice hence
        And leave thy house sans further argument?         90

Lanyon  E'en as thou shalt. I will not bar thy way.

Hyde               If thou preferest, I shall leave thee e'en
                   As thou wert, neither more rich nor more poor.
                   Or, if thou choosest, I shall ope to thee
                   New provinces of knowledge thou know'st not—        95
                   An avenue to fame and power such
                   That thine own eyes shall witness miracles
                   To stagger even Satan's unbelief.

Lanyon             Thy words are banquet most fantastical,
                   With just so many dishes strange. Methinks          100
                   No marvels thou perform'st could shake my faith,
                   Yet I have come too far in this endeavor
                   To pause ere I have seen it to the end.

Hyde               'Tis well. Remember, Lanyon, all thy vows:
                   What follows is protected by the seal               105
                   Of our profession. Thou, who holdest fast
                   Unto thy narrow and materials views,
                   Denied the field of higher medicine,
                   Derided thy superiors—behold!

*[Hyde drinks the tincture and convulses. As he changes, he is concealed from the*
*audience.*

Lanyon             O God above, what fresh new hell is this?           110
                   Who is thus bold to overturn thy plans?
                   When turn'd our souls away from nature's art?
                   How fell we so, inventing sins anew?
                   Where in the depths seek we creation's pow'r?
                   Why at our human strivings dost thou heckle?        115
                   The man is Hyde no more, 'tis Henry Jekyll!

*[Exeunt.*

## SCENE 3.
*Lanyon's residence, days later.*

*Enter GABRIEL JOHN UTTERSON.*

| | | |
|---|---|---|
| Utterson | What days of simple joy are mine of late, | |
| | With nothing to disrupt the quiet calm. | |
| | A fortnight hence I din'd at Henry's home, | |
| | With Hastie there to make the party three, | |
| | Our trio—Jekyll, Lanyon, Utterson— | 5 |
| | United once again, as if the sad | |
| | Events of bygone days had ne'er occurr'd. | |
| | What lightness of the spirit now is mine, | |
| | As if I could sprout wings and fly away. | |
| | The only wrinkle in the fabric pure | 10 |
| | Is that no word from Henry I've receiv'd, | |
| | Though I have, many times now, call'd on him. | |
| | Thus, presently, I come to call on Hastie, | |
| | To see what he may know of Jekyll's state. | |

*He knocks. Enter HASTIE LANYON, standing in the doorway.*

| | | |
|---|---|---|
| Lanyon | Good morning, Gabriel. | |
| | | |
| Utterson |       —Hastie, art thou well? | 15 |
| | *[Aside:]* The answer, though, is writ before mine eyes: | |
| | The man of rosy cheek hath grown most pale, | |
| | His flesh doth fall away, and he appears | |
| | Much balder and far older than when last | |
| | We met, death's warrant on his face inscrib'd. | 20 |
| | Belike, as doctor, he is well aware | |
| | How threadbare is the cord of his own fate, | |
| | Soon, by the sisters three, to be cut short. | |
| | The knowledge may be more than he can bear. | |
| | | |
| Lanyon | Thine aspect gives away thine ev'ry thought. | 25 |
| | Thou seest on me the chill of death's embrace. | |
| | | |
| Utterson | The change o'er thee is most apparent, friend. | |

74

Lanyon  A shock I've had, from which I'll ne'er recover.
     My life is numberèd in weeks or days,
     Yet, for all that, 'twas an abundant life,   30
     Which gave me cause for wonder and delight.
     Methinks, though, if we humans could know all,
     We should be all the gladder to depart.

Utterson  I gather Jekyll hath been ill as well;
     No word have I from him. Hast thou seen Henry? 35

Lanyon  The name of Doctor Jekyll speak thou not.
     I wish no more to see or hear of him.
     That person I regard as dead and gone.

Utterson  Tut! Can it be? Have you so fallen out
     That friendship's bonds may never be restor'd? 40
     We three are old friends, Hastie, and shall not
     Live long enow to foster friendships new.

Lanyon  Naught can be done. If thou wouldst know wherefore,
     Thou mayst, of him, make enquiry direct.

Utterson  On him I've call'd, but no reply receiv'd.   45

Lanyon  Most unsurprising. After I am dead,
     Perhaps thou shalt unveil the right and wrong
     That doth endure twixt Henry and myself.
     More I'll not say. If thou wouldst come and sit,
     And speak to me of other things than these,  50
     Of days more pleasing, subjects cheerier,
     Of those few somethings taking up thy time,
     Of those sweet nothings playing on thy soul,
     Of all the yon and hither of thy life,
     This would I gladly hear, and many hours  55
     Enjoy thy most enriching company.
     Stay clear of that one topic most accurs'd
     And thou art welcome, friend—long as thou lik'st.

*Enter MESSENGER.*

| | | |
|---|---|---|
| Messenger | Beg pardon, sirs, I have a message for<br>A Mister Utterson. | |
| Utterson | —Yea, I am he. | 60 |
| Messenger | Your butler, sir, said I might find you here.<br>I have a letter of some great import,<br>With firm instruction to deliver it<br>Wheree'er you are, at home or whereabout.<br>Thus have I hither follow'd you in haste. | 65 |
| Utterson | Pray render me the letter, then, at once. | |

*[The messenger hands Utterson a letter.*

| | |
|---|---|
| Messenger | Good day, sir. |
| Utterson | —Many thanks for thy resolve. |

*[Exit messenger.*

| | | |
|---|---|---|
| Lanyon | Who writes to thee with such an urgent pen? | |
| Utterson | The answers to the questions I would ask<br>Come, like Pheidippides, on swiftest feet.<br>I'll wager this is Henry's handwriting. | 70 |
| Lanyon | My curiosity o'ercomes my sense;<br>I'd hear the letter if thou art inclin'd. | |
| Utterson | We'll shall, together, learn what he doth say.<br>*[Reading:]* "Dear Gabriel, much have I to say to thee.<br>I have receiv'd thy many messages,<br>And with regret have giv'n them no response.<br>Know this: our old friend Lanyon and myself<br>Have had a rift that nothing may repair.<br>He will not meet me, and I share his view.<br>From henceforth, I shall lead a life mark'd by | 75<br><br><br><br><br>80 |

Extreme seclusion. Be thou not surpris'd,
Nor doubt my friendship, if my door is shut
Forevermore e'en to such friends as thou,
But suffer me to go my lonesome way.                    85
Upon myself I've brought a punishment
And danger far beyond what I may name.
The sinners and the sufferers alike
Shall call me chief, for well I know their plights.
Ne'er did I think God's good earth could contain       90
So many terrors to unman me so.
But one thing mayst thou do to give me aid:
Respect my silence wholly, Utterson,
And seek me not where I may not be found."

Lanyon          O dark and tragic words.

Utterson                —Whate'er thou know'st              95
I shall not force from thee, for friendship's sake,
But Hastie, prithee: ere thou breath'st thy last,
Give me to know how this foul rift began.
Alas, my mood for visiting hath wan'd
E'en as my worry waxeth. Fare thee well.                100

Lanyon          Perhaps in better times we'll meet again.
                                        *[Exit Utterson.*
Such time, howe'er, may be at heaven's gates,
Where on the judgment day we three shall stand
Before Saint Peter and recount our lives—
Kind Utterson, bold Jekyll, fearful Lanyon.             105
Upon that day, what answer will we make?
Shall we, by grace, make entry into heav'n
Despite our roles in such corrupt events?
Or shall we unto hell below be sent
For countering the order natural?                       110
Such abstract questions, for the nonce, are moot,
Yet shall for me, anon, become acute.

                                        *[Exit.*

## SCENE 4.
### *A street.*

*Enter GABRIEL JOHN UTTERSON, holding a letter.*

| | |
|---|---|
| Utterson | A fortnight later, Doctor Lanyon died. |
| | This very morn the fun'ral rites were said, |
| | And now toward my office am I bound. |
| | Along the way, this letter shall I ope, |
| | Penn'd hastily by Hastie's trembling hand, |
| | And superscribed emphatic'lly as "Private: |
| | Writ for the eyes of Utterson alone, |
| | And should he die ere me, to be destroy'd." |
| | One friend already have I lost today— |
| | What if the letter should cost me another |
| | By what, sans doubt, it shall reveal of Jekyll? |

*[He opens the envelope.*

Like nesting dolls, where one doth ope to show
Its twin within, another envelope
Awaits inside, with these few words upon't:
*[Reading:]* "Not to be open'd till the ill-tim'd death
Or disappearance of one Henry Jekyll."
These selfsame words did Jekyll write upon
His will, which caus'd me consternation much.
By his admission, 'twas the bold idea
Of sinister, vile Hyde; but that e'en Lanyon
Should hap upon the thought of Jekyll's death
Or disappearance—O, what should this mean?
Professional responsibility
Requireth that I set this note aside
And leave it for another tragic day,
Should that unfortunate day e'er arrive.
Zounds! Answers slip, like water, from my grasp,
And only questions resolute remain.

*Enter POOLE.*

| | |
|---|---|
| Poole | Good afternoon, dear Mister Utterson. |
| | This morn, I saw you at the funeral |
| | Of Doctor Lanyon, where I sat withal |

Line numbers: 5, 10, 15, 20, 25, 30

|          | The serving class, behind you in the church. |    |
|          | Methought the ceremony was most stirring.    |    |

| Utterson | Poole! Like an emissary from the gods,          |    |
|          | Thou comest at the time of greatest need,       | 35 |
|          | For Lanyon's rites do fill me with grave thoughts |  |
|          | And questions would I ask of thee anon.         |    |

| Poole    | I am, sir, at your service utterly.             |    |

| Utterson | Some two weeks hence a message I receiv'd       |    |
|          | Sent by thy master, which inform'd me of        | 40 |
|          | His fix'd intention to, henceforward, lead      |    |
|          | A life secluded from society.                   |    |

| Poole    | The note I noted well, and it was I             |    |
|          | Who call'd upon the messenger who brought it.   |    |

| Utterson | Doth his intentions match his missive bold?     | 45 |
|          | Were I to call on Jekyll at his home,           |    |
|          | Would I admittance be permitted?                |    |

| Poole    |             —Nay.                               |    |
|          | Alas, I have instruction, sir, to bar           |    |
|          | All visitors and comers to our door.            |    |

| Utterson | His actions accurately suit his words.          | 50 |
|          | Canst tell me aught, Poole? Is thy master well? |    |

| Poole    | To claim his wellness or the lack thereof       |    |
|          | Is more than I can confidently say.             |    |
|          | He doth confine himself e'en from his servants, |    |
|          | Deep in the bowels of his lab'ratory.           | 55 |
|          | I have not seen his face these fourteen days,   |    |
|          | For he doth spend his waking hours within       |    |
|          | And often sleepeth midst his instruments.       |    |
|          | In sooth, he groweth silent dreadfully,         |    |
|          | More out of spirits and unlike himself          | 60 |
|          | Than I have known in years of serving him.      |    |
|          | He reads not, studies not, far as I know,       |    |

|  | |  |
|---|---|---|
|  | Yet seemeth, by the weight of his own thoughts— | |
|  | Which burden him like heavy-loaded mule— | |
|  | To be consum'd by matters of the mind. | 65 |
|  | Whole days shall pass wherein he hardly moves, | |
|  | Or eats, or drinks, or liveth aught of life. | |
| Utterson | Hast ever known thy master to be so? | |
| Poole | This mood is chang'd, his humor turns to woe. | |
| Utterson | Shalt thou not be convinc'd to let me in? | 70 |
| Poole | Nay. O'er my pity doth my duty win. | |
| Utterson | Unto the last art thou most loyal, Poole. | |
| Poole | I fear it maketh me an errant fool. | |
| Utterson | Come, wilt thou walk with me as equals do? | |
|  | The birds do sing, the sky still shineth blue, | 75 |
|  | Perchance a walk shall light a sullen mood. | |
| Poole | Lead onward, that we both may be renew'd. | |

*[Exeunt.*

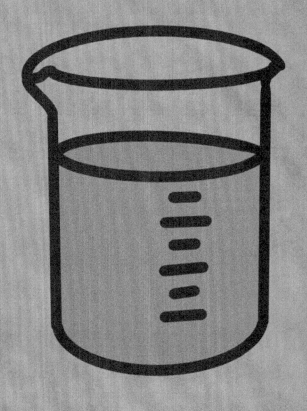

# ACT V

# SCENE 1.

### *The street near Jekyll's residence.*

*Enter RICHARD ENFIELD.*

| | | |
|---|---|---|
| Enfield | 'Tis Sunday come again, and this the spring— | |
| | Though morning's light is darken'd by grim clouds, | |
| | And angels of the night have hid their faces— | |
| | Yet we endure the weather's treachery, | |
| | Myself and dear old Utterson walk on, | 5 |
| | Whose mood hath been as changing as the moon | |
| | For many weeks, in trying times as these. | |

*Enter GABRIEL JOHN UTTERSON.*

| | | |
|---|---|---|
| Utterson | Good morrow, Richard. | |
| Enfield |       —Gabriel, shall we walk? | |
| Utterson | Yea, but, I pray, let's take a newfound route. | |
| | There is a street nearby I long to see, | 10 |
| | Whose cobbles are, methinks, a welcome change | |
| | From that well-trodden path of weekly wont. | |
| Enfield | E'en as you say. *[They walk.]* And now, to late events, | |
| | It seemeth Mister Hyde is vanquish'd quite, | |
| | And never shall I see his face again, | 15 |
| | Which did affright me when I first beheld it. | |
| Utterson | Mine earnest hope is that thy words prove true. | |
| | Did I tell thee that I espied him once, | |
| | And felt the selfsame loathing for him that | |
| | Was thine immediate impression too? | 20 |

| Enfield | To see him was to be repuls'd by him— |
|---|---|
| | It seems the one is partner to the other. |
| | Yet, where is this thy cunning feet have led? |
| | Dost thou believe I would not recognize |
| | The hidden route to Doctor Jekyll's street? |

25

| Utterson | A pretense that I hope thou wilt forgive— |
|---|---|
| | Indeed, I knew full well where we were bound. |
| | Perchance, though, since we two have here arriv'd, |
| | Unto the courtyard we may slyly step |
| | And, thereupon, into the windows peer. |

30

In troth, I am uneasy for poor Henry.
E'en out of doors, the presence of a friend
May offer him some little benefit.

Enfield      Thou art a worthy, sympathetic man.

*Enter HENRY JEKYLL on balcony, at his window.*

| Utterson | Lo, there he sitteth, by the window pane— |
|---|---|

35

How he doth take the air most solemnly,
With sadness infinite upon his mien,
As if he were not resting in his home
But some confin'd, discons'late prisoner.
*[Calling:]* Ho, Jekyll! Art thou well? How is thy health? 40
Dost thou improve e'en as the seasons change?

Jekyll      Forgive me, Utterson, I saw thee not.
I am quite low, like Ark beneath the flood.
My consolation is: it shall not last.

| Utterson | Too much of the indoors hast thou endur'd. |
|---|---|

45

Come out with Mister Enfield and myself—
He is my cousin, and we two are bound
Upon our Sunday walk, would welcome thee
As we stir up the humors in the blood,

|          |                                                          |    |
|----------|----------------------------------------------------------|----|
|          | Restoring our tir'd bodies in a trice.                   | 50 |
|          | Come with us, prithee—bring thy hat and coat             |    |
|          | And take a turn about the area.                          |    |

Jekyll    Thou art most kind to urge thy company—
          Would I thine invitation could accept.
          Alas, the journey is impossible.                           55
          I dare not walk about in public view.
          Thy visit, to a sin-sick soul, is balm.

Utterson  Then we shall pause our stroll, remain below,
          And speak to thee as courtyard stones give ear.

Jekyll    Delightful shall that be in ev'ry—nay!                     60
          *[In Hyde's voice:]* Be gone at once and darken not this door!
          *[In his own voice:]* Leave, friends, afore some terror
                                              comes o'er ye!

Enfield   What is this sudden transformation that
          So speedily doth seize his common sense?

Utterson  May God forgive us—God forgive us all!                     65

                              *[Exeunt Utterson and Enfield, afeard.*

Jekyll    Thus comfort comes and, thus, in fear departs.
          How, like a penitent, my bleak mind turns
          E'en to confession of what none doth know:
          Sooth, Hyde and Jekyll are the selfsame man,
          The twofold incarnation of one soul.                       70
          Rare and unusual experiments
          Allow'd my baser, evil side to have
          New life, but being less robust than my
          Good nature, thus a diff'rence came to pass:
          Edward Hyde is a shorter man than Jekyll.                   75

Cold, surly, and repugnant is his mien;
All those who see him feel their hearts recoil.
Since my first transformation unto Hyde,
Espying his face in my looking-glass,
Oft have I shudder'd at Hyde's evils and                 80
Found succor in converting back to Jekyll.
Despair o'ercomes me at the acts of Hyde,
Regret—though Jekyll hath no share of blame—
Just I remain, though Hyde is most unjust.
Each time I took the tincture, I crav'd more,            85
Kept adding to it—double, and once treble—
Yea, slowly did my better self thus fade.
Like wine that turneth unto vinegar,
Lo, one day did I find myself transform'd
And Hyde was there, though no draught had I drunk. 90
Next, Hyde did murder innocent Carew,
Destroying utterly my life and his—
My evil side thus conquerèd the good,
Ran rampant o'er my scientific pow'rs.
How often, now, I go to sleep as Jekyll,                 95
Yet wake as Hyde, who claims my life as his.
Death is the only answer that remains,
Escape from all my grievous sins and pains.

*[Exit.*

## SCENE 2.
*Night. Jekyll's residence.*

*Enter GABRIEL JOHN UTTERSON.*

Utterson       Some two weeks hath it been since I, with Enfield,
Spake unto Jekyll neath his window pane.
At Poole's entreaty have I come again—
Some trouble, which will not wait for the morn.

The pale moon, as if veilèd by the wind,                    5
Doth hide tonight. Will it presage some doom?

*Enter POOLE.*

Poole            My thanks, dear sir, for coming in a trice.

Utterson        Thine urgent summons I receivèd, Poole,
                And hither have I come with utmost haste.
                Pray, to the matter, whate'er it may be.                    10

Poole            You know the ways of Doctor Jekyll, sir,
                How—like a clam that hideth in its shell,
                Which for the fear of foes will not be rous'd—
                The doctor shuts himself away completely.
                So hath he in his lab'ratory stay'd                    15
                A full week now—yet, sir, I am afeard.

Utterson        Pray tell what it is that thou dost fear,
                And if I can bring comfort to thy ship—
                Which even now is toss'd upon the waves
                And buffeted by stormy gales—I shall.                    20

Poole            Yea, such a tempest overtakes my hull
                That I fear drowning. I suspect foul play.

Utterson        Foul play? This is an unexpected squall.

Poole            Pray, come along, and you shall witness all,
                I—first mate to the captain of the ship—                    25
                Shall be most glad if you see naught but calm
                Upon the troubl'd face of Jekyll's sea.

Utterson        Lead on, and I shall follow after thee.

*Enter RUTH, joining them.*

| | | |
|---|---|---|
| Utterson | Ruth, welcome to this conference of care. | |
| Ruth | We are most grateful for your coming, sir. | 30 |
| Utterson | Dost thou not serve the home of Mister Hyde? | |
| Ruth | The man hath fled, abandoning his home, | |
| | Thus to my rightful place have I return'd. | |
| | Though here I find that fair is turn'd to foul, | |
| | Serenity to dread and calm to panic. | 35 |

*[They walk to the laboratory door.*

| | | |
|---|---|---|
| Poole | I prithee, sir, come gently as you can | |
| | And exercise the power of your ears. | |
| | Pray, listen at the door and—should he ask— | |
| | I bid you enter not, for your own sake. | |

*[Poole knocks on the door.*

*[Calling:]* Sir, Mister Utterson is come for you.  40

*HENRY JEKYLL, as EDWARD HYDE, is concealed behind the door.*

| | |
|---|---|
| Hyde | *[within:]* I prithee tell him I'll see no one, Poole. |
| Poole | E'en as you wish, sir. I bid you good night. |

*[Poole leads Utterson and Ruth away from the door.*

| | |
|---|---|
| Ruth | Sir, you must hear. Was that our master's voice? |
| Utterson | Indeed, it seems much chang'd. |
| Poole | —Chang'd! Verily, |

For twenty years have I serv'd in this house— 45
Should I, then, fail to recognize his voice?
Nay, sir, my master hath been borne away!
'Tis eight days since; we heard him cry for God—
Most horrible and anguish'd was the shout,
Which stirr'd in us profuse, soul-shaking fright— 50
The rest was silence. Yet, for days thereafter,
Another voice doth daily moan to heav'n—
Or mayhap hell, whence wickèd demons come—
Though who is there, if it be not my master,
And wherefore it remaineth, I know not. 55

Utterson    Most strange, Poole, like a tale for rainy nights,
Where fancy and a joy in fear hold sway.
Supposing Doctor Jekyll had been kill'd,
Which is the inference thou boldly mak'st,
What should induce the murderer to stay? 60
It standeth not the test of reason, Poole.

Ruth    Behold, we've reasons past all reasoning.
Whatever meals that have been eaten by
The resident therein were ta'en by stealth,
Yea, pilfer'd from the kitchen's ample stores. 65
Whoever doth reside beyond that door
Doth cry, like keening calf or howling wolf,
And asketh for a sort of medicine
That doth, we know not why, elude the man.
Our master's wont, when he was hard at work, 70
Was to give us instructions by his pen,
Which he would slip beneath the chamber door
So as to keep his efforts undisturb'd.
Naught but instructions have we this past week,
Which fly from underneath the door like wasps, 75
Each one unto our eyes a short, sharp sting.
These papers—coming twice and thrice each day—

Demand some mixtures from apothecaries
All over London. Yet, when Poole and I
Return with utmost haste, deliv'ring them,                    80
They are sent back, with orders to return,
For they are found impure, not strong enow.
The proper drug is wanted bitterly.

Utterson          Have you yet any sample of these papers?

                                                    *[Poole produces a note.*

Poole             Behold one giv'n beneath the door today.        85

Utterson          *[reads:]* "Fair greetings unto ye, the Misters Maw,
                  From Doctor Henry Jekyll, whom you know.
                  The potions that you sent of late have prov'd
                  Impure and useless for my present purpose.
                  Last year, I had abundant quantity              90
                  From ye, which was the finest stock indeed.
                  I beg ye, now, to search with zealous care,
                  And, finding any of the selfsame stuff,
                  Pray send it by my servant Poole anon.
                  Expense is no consideration, sirs.              95
                  Th'importance unto Doctor Jekyll is
                  Impossible to overstate, in sooth."
                  *[Aside:]* So far the letter seemeth sensible,
                  But at the end the writing runneth wild,
                  The pen a-splutter darkly o'er the paper,       100
                  And in a blotch the final words are writ:
                  *[Reading:]* "For God's sake, find me some touch of
                                                          the old."
                  *[To Poole:]* A letter most unusual, forsooth.
                  How is it that you still possess the note,
                  If unto Misters Maw it was deliver'd?           115

Poole          The elder Mister Maw threw it at once
Back in my face, an 'twere a clod of dirt.

Utterson      Thou must see this is Jekyll's handwriting?

Ruth           Yea, sir, and yet that matters not a whit,
For we have seen the beast who waits within.    120
'Twas yesterday, as I came from the garden.
He must have wander'd out to find the drugs,
And stood there, at the far end of the room,
Engag'd in pawing o'er his boxes old
Like rats who search through refuse for their food.  125
When he saw me, gave he a kind of yelp,
And quickly to the lab'ratory ran.
One moment only did I see his face,
A time enow to set my hair a-prickle.
If 'twere my master, why wore he a mask?    130
If 'twere my master, why cry like a pup?
If 'twere my master, why flee from my sight?

Utterson      'Tis odd, I grant, yet reason holds its sway:
Thy master is seiz'd by a malady
That tortures and deforms the sufferer.    135
The alteration of his normal voice,
The swift avoidance of his household staff,
The eagerness with which he'd find the drugs,
The hope for ultimate recovery—
This matter hath an explanation clear,    140
And saves us from exorbitant alarm.

Ruth           That thing was not my master, by my troth.
My master doth possess a tall, fine frame,
Yet this foul imp stood smaller than my waist.

| | | |
|---|---|---|
| Utterson | *[aside:]* That final detail sets my heart to shake, | 145 |
| | For it doth bear the marks of Edward Hyde. | |
| | *[To Ruth:]* If thou hold'st to these words, we must | |
| | be sure. | |
| | Though I would spare your master's privacy, | |
| | And though this note proclaims he liveth still, | |
| | My duty 'tis to break the chamber door. | 150 |
| | | |
| Poole | Ah, Mister Utterson, you speak with sense! | |
| | | |
| Utterson | Yet who shall do the deed? | |
| | | |
| Poole | —We three, at once. | |
| | There is an axe within the scullery. | |
| | | |
| Ruth | And I shall fetch a poker from the fire. | |

*[They leave and return with the instruments.*

| | | |
|---|---|---|
| Utterson | In peril hereby do we place ourselves, | 155 |
| | And—like a soldier on a battlefield, | |
| | Who could be first to strike, yet knoweth that | |
| | The action doth incite a deadly war— | |
| | We must be circumspect. The person, Ruth: | |
| | Was it a man whom thou didst recognize? | 160 |
| | | |
| Ruth | It quickly 'scaped and doublèd up itself, | |
| | Yet if you ask if it was Mister Hyde, | |
| | Mine answer, sir, is yea: methinks it was. | |
| | The stature and the movement were the same, | |
| | And he has access to the lab'ratory, | 165 |
| | For at the time when Sir Carew was slain | |
| | He had the entry key upon him still. | |
| | Yet there is more: did you meet Mister Hyde? | |

Utterson     I met him once.

Ruth             —Then surely you must know
That there was something chilling in the man,    170
A feeling in the marrow, cold and thin,
Which set upon the bones of all who met him.

Utterson     The feeling thou describest I know well.

Ruth     The selfsame feeling, like a lightning bolt,
Shot through my spine as I beheld the man.    175
In troth, this is not evidence enow,
Yet, by my soul, I know 'twas Mister Hyde.

Utterson     Long have I fear'd some evil would arise
From Jekyll's close connection unto Hyde.
Now I suspect that Henry hath been kill'd,    180
And his foul murderer awaits within—
Still lurking in his victim's workroom—for
What darker purpose God alone doth know.
Come, let our name be vengeance, verily.
*[Calling:]* Hear, Jekyll: I demand to see thee now!    185
I tell thee, our suspicions are arous'd—
Fair warning have I giv'n, and tell thee plainly:
I must and shall see thee, whatever comes,
If not by thy consent, then by brute force!

Hyde     *[within:]* Nay Utterson, be merciful, by God.    190

Ruth     How he doth weep, e'en like a poor, lost soul.
I could weep, too, the voice doth move me so.

Utterson     But 'tis not Jekyll's voice—'tis Hyde's, I'll wager!
Down with the door, for we shall see his face!

*[They begin hammering at the door and break it down.*

Poole        The deed is done! We enter!

Ruth            —O, the horror!               195

*[They find Hyde, twitching on the ground.*

Utterson    The papers are set forth most orderly,
The chemicals all in their places, too—
'Twould be the calmest room in Christendom
Except for he who lieth on the ground.
'Tis Edward Hyde, and yet the clothes he wears    200
Are far too large for him and his small frame.

Ruth         O, how he doth contort and wildly shakes.

Poole        These are the pangs of death, undoubtedly.

Utterson    Behold the vial still within his hand,
The smell of tincture present on the air:        205
The man hath slain himself. We come too late
To save or capture, either. It remains
To find the body of your master true.

*[They search the laboratory.*

Poole        There's neither hide nor hair of Doctor Jekyll.
Perhaps he's buried underneath the stones.     210

Utterson    Or may have fled.

Ruth              —Nay, sirs, here lies the answer:
'Tis Doctor Jekyll's will and testament.

| | |
|---|---|
| Poole | Please, Mister Utterson, unseal the will. |
| Utterson | What if poor Henry liveth even now? |
| | Should we reveal his final worldly wishes?      215 |
| Ruth | The will is to be open'd in the case |
| | Of Doctor Jekyll's death or disappearance. |
| | The one is still unproven, but the second |
| | Is certain as his absence from this room. |
| Utterson | Thou reason'st like a cunning lawyer, Ruth.      220 |
| Poole | I beg you, sir, to ope and read the will. |
| Utterson | I fear; God grant I have no cause for it. |

                                         *[He opens the will.*

                    *[Reads:]* "Dear Utterson, if thou read'st this farewell,

                    I shall have disappear'd or gone to die.

                    Though what the future holds I cannot tell,      225

                    Mine instinct tells me that the end is nigh.

                    Hear now the bold confession of thy friend,

                    Unhappy Henry Jekyll, at his end."

| | |
|---|---|
| Ruth | *[reads:]* "Long have I search'd to cleave myself in twain— |
| | Let good be wholly good, sans disputation,      230 |
| | Set evil free to reign o'er its domain— |
| | And sought, against the nature of creation, |
| | To bring about a separation full |
| | Through scientific means—such was my goal." |
| Poole | *[reads:]* "'Twas many months ago when I, at length,   235 |
| | Put theory to the test and—having mix'd |
| | The tincture to the perfect blend and strength— |
| | Sipp'd of the cup that, soon, my fortune fix'd. |
| | I felt my body change, and I espied, |

Within my looking-glass, the face of Hyde."    240

Utterson    *[reads:]* "Yea, I am he—of that make no mistake,
When he was present, evil walk'd alone,
And did the deeds that made all London shake,
For which I ever felt I must atone.
Th'assault of that young lass was Hyde's first coup,    245
The final was the murder of Carew."

Ruth    *[reads:]* "I was to blame and yet was not to blame,
The actions were not mine, and yet they were.
When I restor'd myself to mine own name,
I felt some guilt for whate'er did occur.    250
In certain instances, I would make right
The wrongdoings that Hyde perform'd by night."

Poole    *[reads:]* "Alas, if fully I'd unburden'd be,
There's more that, unto thee, I must admit:
I revel'd in rank Hyde's offensive spree,    255
The worse he was, the more I long'd for it.
Soon, ev'ry night my soul would feel the tug
To taste the rapture of the thrilling drug."

Utterson    *[reads:]* "This shall explain the change unto my will
That rightfully upset thee, Utterson.    260
The matter vex'd me frightfully, until
I saw no other way it could be done:
If Hyde should somehow be the one to live,
It seem'd I must, to him, my holdings give."

Ruth    *[reads:]* "We come to the conclusion of my tale:    265
The horrid end from innocent beginning.
Though I tried remedies to no avail,
For weeks Hyde came—sans draught—to do his sinning.
Though firmly I resolv'd no more to change,

                Hyde's power did my steadfastness outrange."      270

Poole        *[reads:]* "Too often, whilst I idly liv'd as Jekyll,
                I suddenly transform'd to Mister Hyde.
                But from th'apothecaries came no speckle
                Of that pure drug that, once, I had applied
                To make myself to mine own form return—     275
                Thus Jekyll froze whilst Hyde made London burn."

Utterson     *[reads:]* "In such a state did hopeless Sir Carew
                Face Hyde and meet the end thou knowest well.
                I called on Lanyon then, who nothing knew,
                In hopes my potions could my troubles quell.    280
                The tinctures he collected cur'd me not:
                And thus, within mine own net am I caught."

Ruth         *[reads:]* "This story must seem fanciful, absurd,
                Thy reason shall it laughably assail.
                Yet I write this confession—true each word—    285
                Secluded from the world: my home my jail,
                For Hyde appeareth now whene'er he will.
                I dare not let him loose, more blood to spill."

Poole        *[reads:]* "Methinks this little room may be my grave,
                The lab'ratory where began my woes.      290
                My hope is Hyde his errant soul shall save—
                Release himself unto death's final throes.
                With this confession, in a sound mind penn'd,
                I bring the life of Jekyll to its end."

Utterson     O strange and curious, past all belief.         295

Ruth         Poor master, how he suffer'd for his notions.

Poole        And, in so doing, set a demon loose.

Utterson    A glooming still this midnight with it brings;
            The moon, for sorrow, will not show its head.
            Go Poole, fetch Newcomen to see these things—    300
            See Jekyll pardon'd, mayhap punishèd.
            For never was a case more vexing tried
            Than Doctor Jekyll and his Mister Hyde.

                                        *[Exeunt omnes.*

# AFTERWORD

*Strange Case of Dr. Jekyll and Mr. Hyde*, by Robert Louis Stevenson, has captured the human imagination. Most people know the basics of the 1886 story—a doctor creates a potion that turns him into a vice-loving criminal—even if they haven't read it. The story became a musical in 1990, and an IMDb search for "Jekyll" produces an astonishing list of movies, TV episodes, and more.

A parody of the story—the Looney Tunes cartoon "Hyde and Hare"—is responsible for my lifelong fascination with Dr. Jekyll and Mr. Hyde, though I didn't read Stevenson's original until I was in my 30s. Reading it in the same year that I wrote the *William Shakespeare's Star Wars* prequel trilogy inspired me to write a Shakespearean trilogy based on classic horror tales. Eight years later, *William Shakespeare's Strange Case of Doctor Jekyll and Mister Hyde*, or *The Modern Janus*, is finally done.

At just over 25,000 words, Stevenson's novella features few characters and a simple plot. The body of Edward Hyde is discovered— and the action of the narrative ends—two-thirds of the way through the book (page 50 of 75 in the Signet Classics edition I own). The final third are the letters of Doctor Lanyon and the confession of Henry Jekyll. All of which is to say: this story is a challenge to adapt.

As when I adapted Mary Shelley's *Frankenstein*, which isn't told in chronological order, I put the narrative into an order that makes dramatic sense rather than literary sense. When Hyde dies in the story, the truth is still a mystery, and it's only the two letters that reveal what happened. On stage, where the same actor plays both Jekyll and Hyde (at least that's how I imagine it, though an argument could be made for separate actors), the secret is harder to keep and the story's climax is more about catching the villain than unraveling the mystery. That's the transition from mystery to horror.

For those reasons, the first scene of the play features portions of Jekyll's confession from the end of the novella, and though the play roughly follows the narrative progression of the first two-thirds of the book, it is sprinkled throughout with revelations from the end. A theatergoer who is completely unfamiliar with the story would be certain, by the middle of Act IV (when Lanyon witnesses the transformation), that Jekyll is Hyde and vice versa, but it's pretty clear by the end of Act I, scene 1. My adaptation focuses less on the mystery than on the horror of evil that is set free and grows past the point of control.

The idea of setting our baser natures free is what gives *Strange Case of Dr. Jekyll and Mr. Hyde* such a prominent place in the cultural imagination. To greater or lesser extents, we've all imagined letting our demons have their day, whether it's a child picturing themselves shouting during a solemn assembly, a businessperson imagining quitting their job in a blaze of glory, or much, much worse. I tried to emphasize the push and pull of good and evil throughout the book, with many characters using opposites to express themselves: "To drink of evil doth increase my thirst, / To feast on sin makes me the hungrier."

A few other notes: The play's subtitle, *The Modern Janus*, is inspired by Mary Shelley's subtitle to *Frankenstein*, which is *The Modern Prometheus*. Janus was the Roman god of gates and doors who had two faces on his head so he could see both before and behind him, seeing who was entering and exiting and, metaphorically, seeing what was to come and what had already been. That's why the month of January is named for Janus; it's the month when we look back at the year that has passed and forward to the year ahead. Janus' two-faced nature is an apt metaphor for Jekyll and Hyde.

Jekyll's letter of confession felt necessary to the final scene, but I didn't want the three characters to just stand there and read a letter. That's why I wrote it in rhyming verse (ABABCC structure, like Shakespeare's poem "Venus and Adonis"). It stands apart as something unique, something out of time with the rest of the play.

None of the women in Stevenson's book are named. In case you're curious, I named Jekyll's servant Ruth after my grandmother and, having done so, named the witness to Sir Carew's murder Edith because Ruth and Edith are two of the sisters in *The Pirates of Penzance*. Those are the only Easter eggs I'll explain; the rest are for you to find.

—June 16, 2022
Portland, Oregon

**Ian Doescher** is the *New York Times* bestselling author of the *William Shakespeare Star Wars* series, the Pop Shakespeare series, the children's poetry collection *I Wish I Had a Wookiee*, and other books. He lives in Portland, Oregon with his spouse Jennifer, teenagers Liam and Graham, and dog Thorfinn. Find Ian online at iandoescher.com.

Made in the USA
Middletown, DE
08 October 2022

12231627R00056